CRIME BOSS BABY

KRISTA LAKES

ZIRCONIA PUBLISHING, INC.

Crime Boss Baby

~

From New York Times bestselling author Krista Lakes, comes a sensual, standalone mafia romance that will have you turning the pages at record speed.

I am a mafia princess.

My family is making me marry a rival crime boss.

At first, I go along with it because it's important to my family. But then I meet *him*.

Dante is dangerous and sexy as sin. I want him physically and mentally. His talented fingers and mouth have me panting for more before he even knows my real name.

But there are parts of my past that can ruin everything. My mother's murderer is catching up to me. If he finds me, he could ruin everything. Not only that, not everyone in Dante's family is as excited about the wedding as they appear.

And then, there's news that both overjoys and terrifies me. I'm pregnant.

Can Dante save me and give me the future we both desire? Or will my past destroy everything and everyone that I care about?

~

I bite my lip and smile, nodding. "Take me, Dante. I'm yours to take as you want."

His eyes darken and he suddenly seems taller. He grabs my hair and pulls me to his desk. I sit on the edge of the wood, arching my back and thrusting out my chest. I want to tempt him. I moan loudly, just wanting nothing but his cock inside of me. He leaves one hand in my hair while the other one begins to hike up my skirt.

He caresses my inner thigh, working his fingers up the sensitive flesh to the cloth of my panties. Without warning, he slips a finger into me. Luckily, I want him bad enough that I have a little lubrication, but not nearly enough to make the penetration pleasurable. I wince. "Careful..." I whine as I look back at him.

He removes his hand and sticks the finger in his mouth, savoring my flavor. His face is emotionless while his eyes burn with a lust I don't recognize. "You said to take you. You sure you want to continue?"

I swallow hard. His erection is huge against my leg. "Yes," I whisper, looking at his pants.

A NOTE TO READERS

If you are an avid reader of Krista Lakes novels, certain passages of this novel may feel familiar to you.

This summer, Kindle Worlds shut down their program and I received the rights to three novellas back. I couldn't just let all that hard work and words just sit on my hard drive doing nothing. There was a story there that was worth telling.

However, I wrote those novellas with characters from another author's head. I couldn't just repackage and sell work with her characters in it. Besides, I had a new story that I wanted to tell.

So, I changed the characters. I changed the setting. I changed the circumstances around their story, as well as the key elements. I added chapters and removed huge chunks of old story line that no longer worked for the new characters.

This is a new story.

My protagonist is no longer an escort. She is the daughter of a power crime syndicate.

My hero is no longer dark and twisted. He is now a mob boss with a caring and wonderful heart.

I added characters. I added a baby. I added so much to the original novellas that it no longer resembles the original that I started with. It is its own story now.

Now, it has a happy ending.

So, some of the words may sound familiar. Some of them may feel like deja vu.

This is a new novel. This is a new story with the gaps filled in by old writing so that I can give my readers a new story. A better story. A love story.

CHAPTER 1

I don't remember much about the accident.

I was only twelve at the time.

My mother's boyfriend took me home and tried to kiss me when he found out my mother wasn't there. He was a powerful man, but I didn't understand that at the time. When I pulled away from him, he hit me. He said he owned me and my mother. He tried again and I punched him. I'd never been so scared in my life. I ran from his car and hid at my neighbor's house.

When I told my mother, she was furious with him. I'd never seen her so angry. She pulled out our suitcases and began tossing things into them.

"Pack a bag. We're going to your aunt's house. Be sure to bring Nan's book," she'd told me, pointing to the small bookshelf in our living room. The book was an heirloom bible, passed down from generation to generation. It never left the shelf, but it was always in our house. I knew we were officially settled somewhere when the bible went up on the shelf.

That's how I knew that this was serious. The bible coming off the shelf meant we were leaving.

If I had known what was going to happen, I would have begged her to stay with me. I would have kept her with me and we would have run away together. Sometimes I blame myself, but I know that I couldn't have known. It wasn't my fault.

It was his.

We were almost packed when she got a phone call. It was him. Her boyfriend. She said she was busy, but he said it would only take a moment. He had something for her. She tried to tell him no, but he wasn't the type of man to take that for an answer.

She shut her suitcase hard enough to shake the bed and called her sister, but this time she kept the door shut. I didn't hear that conversation.

"Remember Nan's book," she said, picking up her purse. "It's important. I have to go do this or he'll chase us forever. I'll be right back."

She kissed my forehead and held me to her, her heart pounding in her chest.

"I love you, pumpkin." Those were her last words to me. "I love you so much."

Then she was gone. She wore a yellow sweater and a soft gray dress. Her dark hair was up in a ponytail.

The next time I saw her was at the morgue. There had been a car accident. They said she hadn't been wearing a seat belt and had been ejected from the car. That didn't make any sense to me. My mother was religious about seat belts. She made sure she wore hers even just driving across the parking lot. She wouldn't even start the car until I had mine buckled.

Even then, something felt wrong about her death. Everyone kept avoiding saying something. My uncle came, but even he couldn't seem to get any information out of them. I knew that he was a powerful businessman, yet everyone seemed to avoid telling him anything.

I was young, but I remember everyone looking nervous. They wouldn't answer any of our questions.

"You're a part of our family now," my Aunt Sophie told me. "You're safe with us."

She'd held my hand when I went to identify my mother. She had the same dark brown hair and nose as my mother. Her eyes were blue instead of brown. She didn't smile as much as my mother, though.

No one told me much about the car accident. I'd watched enough crime shows to know that someone should have wanted to speak with me about what happened, but no one ever came.

Now that I'm older, I think I know why.

Senator John Norwood murdered my mother and paid to have it covered up.

~

Ten years after the accident...

"The boss doesn't like you being here," Ethan says, crossing his arms. The muscles flex under his long sleeved t-shirt.

"Well, then he shouldn't have put my name on the lease," I reply, closing the door to the warehouse and making sure it locks. "I'm the one who has to answer the security company calls when the alarm goes off."

Ethan looks around the deserted warehouse parking lot. "You could have called me."

I sigh and cross my arms. "I did. You were busy."

Ethan isn't blood family, but he is family. My uncle took him in when Ethan got out of the military and had no where to go. My uncle needed reliable muscle, and Ethan provides that plus enough common sense to make him valuable.

He's big, strong, scary, and loyal to my aunt and uncle. He treats me like a big brother who has to babysit all the time. I feel like I'm a two year old kid that needs constant supervision the way he watches out for me sometimes.

He glares at me, but I don't back down. Just because he has ten years and fifty pounds of muscle on me, I won't let him intimidate me. He could beat me in a fight with both hands tied behind his back. I know he's deadly. Still, I'm not about to show any weakness.

"Besides, it was nothing. The sensor just didn't fit right. Again," I tell him. I know that we've both walked around the place twice. Nothing is missing. Nothing is out of place. This is the third time this week this exact sensor has done this.

"You know I'm still telling the boss," Ethan says. Always loyal to the family.

"You think I won't?" I ask, raising my eyebrows. "I always tell him. That's probably why he put my name on the lease. If he'd just let me replace the sensor, then we wouldn't have to deal with this crap."

Ethan just glares at me.

"What are you doing out here anyway?" I ask. It's a cold November afternoon in New York. There's snow coming later tonight and I can feel the temperature dropping already. I want to get back to the city. "When I called earlier, you said you were busy. Now you're not?"

"Your aunt wants to see you."

I try not to make a face, but obviously fail. Ethan chuckles.

"Don't let her see that face," he tells me.

I love my aunt. She's a strong woman who taught me my place in the world. But she's a ball buster. She's all business all the time. I like seeing her for Thanksgiving and family related things, but work related business always makes me feel like I've screwed up somewhere. She's the exact opposite of my mother, who was always all about family and business second.

"You need to come with me," Ethan tells me. There's no arguing with him, so I don't even try.

I test the locks one last time, making sure that everything is secure. There are mattresses in this warehouse. They aren't easy to steal, but I'm not taking any chances. I know it's just a flaky sensor, but we have competition that would love to find our warehouse with open doors.

"What does she want?" I ask, following Ethan to his car. I notice that Frankie, the guy who drove me here, already bailed. He probably saw Ethan and took off before he could get in trouble for bringing me to the warehouse. I couldn't blame him. Frankie was low on the totem pole. I wasn't.

"I didn't ask," Ethan says, getting into the drivers seat of his black sedan. The windows are tinted to almost illegal darkness, but I doubt he ever gets pulled over for it. "But she seemed like she was in a good mood."

"Really?" I shrug, putting on my seat belt. I give Ethan a pointed look until he puts his on as well. "Maybe she just wants to give me the leftover turkey from Thanksgiving."

"Don't bet on it."

The tires grind on the gravel as we leave the warehouse behind. I sigh and resign myself to my fate.

CHAPTER 2

The FBI would classify my family's business as an organized crime syndicate. Given that I've seen the filing system my uncle prefers to use, I'd hesitate to call us organized.

Still, our business is on the shady end. We launder money. We organize online sports betting and gambling. We have escort services that provide services that aren't exactly legal in this state. We have interesting goods come through our warehouses that may or may not be legal.

We run it all through our mattress company. It's the perfect cover. Mattresses are big and expensive. The profit margin is huge on a mattress and it allows us to have access to the docks and warehouses. It's the perfect money laundering company. No one asks questions about mattresses.

As far as most people are concerned, we're mattress moguls. As long as you don't look at the books, that's where my family's money comes from. If you look at the books, mattresses don't make much money.

My aunt however is a mobster with morals. We don't deal with drugs. We don't deal in people. No children, no murder for hire, no slavery. My aunt won't work with those that do. She makes sure the escorts are all well taken care of. In her eyes, they are just doing a job and deserve to be paid and treated as such. She makes sure that a portion of our profits are always donated back into the community and to gambling addiction help centers. There are legal companies with less moral standing than my family.

We're not legal, but we're not evil, either.

The Savio family has been in the "mattress" business for generations. It wasn't always mattresses, but always something just a little less than legal with a legal cover. We aren't the biggest or most famous crime family, but we are one of the richest. We were one of the first into online gambling and it has paid off in spades.

My cousin Vinnie is a computer genius. He created one of the best programs for online sports betting as well as online poker games. He did it right as the internet opened up the options. With the mattress stores, we're able to safely launder all of that money.

My uncle and aunt are the head of the Savio family. They adopted me and I'm their only child. I've been trained since I was twelve how to run this business. It's in my blood. It's who I am.

I am a mob princess.

Ethan walks into my aunt's office before I do. I'm glad it's warmer in here. My coat isn't heavy enough for the cold of the day. I can hear my aunt talking on the phone, obviously wooing a customer. I stand outside, waiting and trying to ignore the glances from the people working in the cubicles surrounding her office. It's all part of the business. The cubicles add legitimacy to our finances. They think they're working for a mattress supply chain.

Aunt Sophia finally hangs up the phone when she realizes Ethan is in her office.

"Is she here? Send her in."

Ethan motions to me and I walk in. Aunt Sophia is fishing through a mess of papers on her desk. She's wearing a tailored dark blue skirt and business jacket. Her dark hair is streaked with silver. She sometimes jokes that it's from having to raise a headstrong girl like me.

"I hear you were at the warehouse." She frowns and my chest tightens a little bit. I don't know how she already knows I was at the warehouse. Somehow, she still makes me feel like I'm twelve years old and need to prove myself.

"The alarm went off. It's that faulty sensor. I know the warehouse is half empty, but if we're going to have a security system, it should at least work most of the time," I tell her.

"Your cousin Danny put it in," she says, sitting down in her office chair. "He's family."

"Yeah, so he should fix it," I reply. She gives me a stern look. Aunt Sophia doesn't like being talked back to like this, but she knows I'm right. Still, I'm not to speak ill of family. I soften my tone. "I'll ask him again."

"He's a little absent minded," Aunt Sophia agrees. She waves her hand through the air as if brushing the topic away. "But that's not why I called you here. Have a seat."

I was hoping that that this meeting was for leftover turkey. Aunt Sophia made really good turkey. Sitting down made my dream of turkey a little less likely.

"Do you love your family?" She folds her hands on the top of her desk.

"Of course I do, Aunt Sophia," I quickly reply. "You know I do."

She nods. "Then I'm going to ask you to prove it. You

have the option to say no. You always have the option to say no, you know that."

Butterflies flutter in my stomach. She's never asked me anything like this before.

"What do you need me to do?" I ask, tugging on the edges of my jacket.

My aunt slides a photo across the desk. The man looking out at me from the picture is handsome. His dark hair hangs loosely over his eyes and he has an almost sarcastic smile on his face. There's a darkness in his eyes that makes me a little nervous. He looks familiar to me.

"That's Dante Russo, heir to the Russo Family."

I do a double take. The Russo family is an old world mafia family. They have power and influence that my family could only dream of. They are rivals, only in the sense that we work in similar legally gray areas. They are much more in the import/export business than we are. Still, we run into problems with them every once in a while. Our two families aren't really friendly. More like wolves that share a border.

I don't know what I could have to do with him. Especially with her asking me to prove my love to my family.

My family doesn't put out assassination hits. At least, not regularly and never on someone like Dante Russo.

"What do you want me to do?" The photo shakes a little in my fingers. I don't want to take out a rival. However, I can't think of another reason why my aunt would be handing me a Russo Family photograph.

"I want you to marry him."

That is not what I was expecting. I nearly drop the photo. "What?"

"The Russos want to join our family to theirs." My aunt stands from her desk and starts walking around her office. "We have the money. They have the prestige. Imagine what doors this will open."

"But you want me to marry him," I repeat. I look down at the photo and can't decide how I feel about this. It's definitely better than having to kill him.

"You of course have a choice," my aunt assures me. "You can always say no."

I don't even bother to roll my eyes. Of course I have the choice to hurt the family and go against their wishes. I have the choice to let down the only people I have ever trusted. I also have the choice to walk around naked in Times Square in the middle of winter.

None of those are really choices.

"Marrying him helps the family?" I ask, picking up the picture and trying to imagine a life with this person. There are arranged marriages all the time. It would certainly make my dating life easier.

Aunt Sophia nods. "Combining the Savio and Russo Families will make us the dominate force on the East Coast. We have the money. They have the connections. Together, we'll be unstoppable. No more dock skirmishes. No more fights. Just more business."

I like the idea. It certainly would be good for the family. With the Russo name backing us, a lot of new money making opportunities open up.

I look at the photo. I could do worse than this man with serious dark eyes. As long as he's kind to me and mine, I can make it work. There are worse marriages out there. I've had my taste of love and it has left me bitter.

I throw caution to the winds. This is my chance to shine for my family.

"Okay. I'll do it."

Aunt Sophia's eyebrows raise. "Really?" She didn't expect me to agree so easily.

"It helps the family," I say, setting down the photo. "I know that you've made sure he's a decent match."

Aunt Sophia nods. "He is. He's mafia, but everyone says he'll treat you right."

That meant that he was dangerous, but not to me. He was my kind of dangerous. Mob dangerous.

"I'll take care of everything." Aunt Sophia takes the photo and places it back in her desk. "You'll meet him in a couple of days. He still has to agree to you."

I grin at her. "Come on, everybody wants me."

My aunt cracks a smile. "There's turkey in the fridge for you." She motions with her head to the small refrigerator in the corner of her office and my smile widens.

"Thanks, Aunt Sophia," I say, standing up.

She offers me her cheek and I give her a kiss. For a moment, the stern boss look fades and for a moment she is my aunt. Those moments are rare these days.

"Go get out of here before your uncle hears you were at the warehouse again," she scolds me, but her voice is kind.

I flash her a grin and grab a Tupperware container full of her delicious turkey before heading out of her office. Ethan is waiting for me.

"See, she did want to give me turkey," I tell him, holding up the container.

He rolls his eyes and walks ahead of me toward the car. I smile at his back and try not to think of what I just agreed to do.

CHAPTER 3

My apartment is on the outskirts of New York City. It's close enough to have all the comforts of the city, but far enough away that the traffic is only mostly horrendous. Ethan drives like a cabbie and gets me home in record time.

I live on the fifth floor of an older building. I love this place. It's nicer than anything me and my mom ever had. I lived with my aunt and uncle in the 'burbs, but I never felt at home there. I like the feel and the noise of the city. I like knowing there are always people around me. It makes me feel safe.

I sink into my couch, closing my eyes. I can only ever relax when I'm here by myself, so naturally, I never have guests over. My place is a mess, but what's truly important is that it is *mine.* I can be myself here and I don't have to be the boss's daughter. There are no expectations.

I open my eyes and look over at the upright piano in the corner of the room. It's my pride and joy. My mother had played professionally. She'd met many famous people, including Senator Norwood, because of her talent with the keys. She was amazing. I remember her giving lessons to neighbor kids and their parent's always being so proud to have been taught by a great pianist. I'm nowhere near that good, but playing it now is my connection to her.

It's just an old upright piano, but I saved and bought it for myself. I keep all my sheet music on a small bookshelf next to it, along with Nan's Bible, just like my mom did. The piano and book make this place really feel like home for me.

I think about playing, but I'm not in the mood. I need an outside distraction. I grab my cell phone out of my purse and hold down the "2" button.

"Hello?" a sleepy sounding voice answers from the other end.

"Sara, it's me! Want to go to the piano bar?"

I hear a big yawn. "Can't. I've got an all-day photo-shoot tomorrow. I'm off the next day, though."

"Come on, you big baby. I'll make sure you get your beauty sleep."

"Last time you said that we ended up staying out all night. I could barely keep my eyes open the next day. Besides, the piano bar is more your thing than mine anyway."

"But Sara-"

"I'm hanging up now. Have a great night." I hear the line go dead.

I sigh and look over at the piano. I've got a day off tomorrow, and I can sleep until noon. I'm going to have a good time tonight.

The piano bar is crowded, but then every bar is crowded in New York. Live music, well dressed people, expensive drinks, this place has it all. I love that it's fancy here. I feel high class. I grab a seat at the bar as soon as I get inside, letting the music wash over me.

The piano is at the other side of the room, but I can already tell it isn't the usual guy at the piano tonight. Whereas the regular guy typically plays some contemporary hits but mostly "Golden Oldies" from the 60s and 70s, this guy is playing nothing but classical music. I close my eyes and listen to a piece I don't recognize, but I can tell he's pouring his entire soul into it. Either this song means something to him or he's a piano prodigy.

When the music stops and the people around me begin to clap, I clap as well, not bothering to open my eyes yet. When I do, I look at the piano player and find I'm looking into dark and serious eyes. They're attached to a handsome face on top of a tall, muscular frame. He must have noticed me as well, even though I'm dressed to blend in with a conservative dark red, sheath dress with sleeves. He stands up and starts making his way toward me. It takes me several moments, but as he gets closer and closer, I recognize that face.

The photo that Aunt Sophia showed me.

The man who doesn't know we're engaged.

And he's walking right toward me.

I almost get up and rush out the door, but instinct takes over. I smile as he approaches me.

"Did you like it?" he asks.

"Like what?" I ask back, feeling playful.

"My piano playing."

I laugh. "Do girls often swoon over your piano playing?"

He shrugs. "It's usually a good start. Bartender." A bartender is right there, quicker than I am ever able to get a drink. "Two of whatever she's having."

"You sure you can afford it?" I ask, looking over his clothing. He's wearing ratty jeans and a well worn t-shirt. This is the kind of place that requires a tie. He is not dressed to be here.

His wry smile never leaves his face. "Maybe I own the place," he says, completely deadpan. I laugh, but then remember what Aunt Sophia told me. *Heir to the Russo family.* It's entirely possible that he does own this place. He looks at me and realizes he's said too much.

"Oh really. How can that be possible when I own this place?" I ask, saving the conversation.

He relaxes, then spreads his hands out in front of him in a shrug. "You caught me. I actually just work for the competition."

"Oooh, a spy," I say.

The bartender finishes our drinks and hands them to the young man, never asking for a tab or accepting any cash.

"If I give you this drink, will you promise not to turn me in?" He looks at me with big brown eyes, and I feel like I can't possibly say no.

"Well, I guess I can let it slide. But, if the real owner comes in here, I'll have to let him know," I say.

"Well, cheers to spies," he says, raising his glass. I tip mine to his, then drink. He takes a sip, then asks, "What's your name?"

"I'm not telling you, James Bond," I reply.

I like him already, but he doesn't know about me. He doesn't know that we aren't supposed to meet for a few more days. I don't want to ruin things. I won't let Aunt Sophia and the family down. I need to play this carefully.

He shrugs. "If I can guess your age, will you tell me your name?"

I shrug back. "By all means."

He takes a step back, looking at me up and down while his hand rests on his chin. His eyes linger in all the right places, staring at my hips, my curves, my breasts. Finally, his gaze goes to my eyes. "Twenty," he says. "They should probably card you."

"Not even close, Bond," I say truthfully.

He shrugs. "I'm not sure I believe you. Let me see your driver's license."

My jaw drops. "I am not showing you my driver's license. You probably just want to see my name."

"Well, either that or your height and weight, but I'll settle for either."

My jaw drops again and I lightly slap his chest. It's a flirty thing to do, and I can't believe I did it. I'm not supposed to be flirting with him yet. "I don't drive anyway, I take taxis everywhere."

"Walking around without a driver's license?" the man asks. "The cops could have a field day with you." He takes another look up and down my body, as if he'd like to have a field day with me right now.

I lift my drink in the air. "I guess you're not the only rebel tonight," I say. He cheers me and takes another drink. I have to think of a name to tell him, so I think of the first Bond girl that pops into my head. "Vesper."

He pauses, then shrugs. "Vesper, huh? Alright, sounds like a fun name for tonight. It matches James Bond."

Again he looks at me with those dark eyes. There are secrets in those eyes. A hint of danger and a whole lot of sexiness. I like the way he looks at me. I like the way my body heats under his gaze.

"Alright, Bond. Tell me, what brings you here to New York?"

"Maybe I've got a hot date," he says.

I bet you do, I think to myself. *You just don't know it yet.*

"Really? Are you meeting her here at the bar?" I ask, mocking a look around.

"I think I just met her," he replies.

That one takes me off guard. If only he knew. I just smile and clink glasses with him again, finishing my drink off. "So, are you going to get back on that piano and play some more?"

"That depends. Will you lay on top of it in that red dress?"

"You know, I'm not just some piece of eye candy. I can probably play better than you can," I lie.

His eyebrows shoot up. I can't tell if he's impressed or if he doesn't believe me. "Then let's go play a duet."

I nod my head, but as soon as I move to stand up from the bar stool, the little voice in the back of my head pipes up. *This is a bad idea*, it says. *He doesn't know who you are. He doesn't know your family. This can end so bad. You are in rival families right now.*

"On second thought, Bond, I'll just sit here and enjoy listening to you play," I say.

His broad shoulders slump for a moment, but his smile returns just as quickly. "Suit yourself. This next one's for you."

He goes back to the piano, cracks his knuckles, and sits down to play. At first I don't recognize the piece. It was something that the usual piano player might play, something that you'd hear on an Oldies station. After a moment, I recognize the chorus. It's the Mission Impossible theme.

After he's done, he gets another round of applause, then walks back over to me. He has a big grin on his face, but I don't really return it. "Aw, come on. You can't be that young that you don't recognize this song."

"I recognized it, but I don't get it," I said.

I frown for a moment and then it dawns on me. I can't believe I didn't get the joke. "It's a spy song."

He chuckles and that grin is back. I know that I should leave. If he doesn't recognize me, then he doesn't know about the engagement yet. Or he's playing with me.

Either way, I should escape while it's still a good option.

"Well, Vesper, are you ready to play a song with me? I think there's still one or two Bond movie songs we can play," he says.

He's very charming. I'm tempted, but as I stand up, I remember why I didn't play with him a moment ago. "I can't. I have a busy day of work tomorrow, and I need to go home," I lie. I turn to walk toward the door.

"Wait," he says, and grabs my elbow. I look at him and for a moment I see a dark desire in his eyes. This is a man who is used to getting what he wants. He's used to power. "What are you doing after work tomorrow?"

I look at his strong body up and down, and I feel compelled to answer. "Nothing."

He smiles and lets go of my arm. "Good. How would you like to hang out with me?"

No! the little voice in my head screams. "Okay," my real voice says, betraying me.

His smile is as broad as I've ever seen a man smile. "Great. Do you live nearby?"

"Near enough," I say. No way I'm going to tell a rival mob member where I live. We aren't married yet.

"I'll meet you here. Six o'clock sound good?"

"Six o'clock sounds fine."

"I'll see you then, Vesper." He smiles, then turns on his heel and heads back to the piano. As he starts to play, he looks right at me, then plays what might as well be a victory fanfare. I laugh, then walk out the door.

Stupid, stupid, stupid, I think to myself. I shouldn't be making this into a bigger thing than it is. Yet his sexy charm has won me over, has made it so I can't even think straight. I can't help but think how nice it might be to date him with family approval.

CHAPTER 4

For a few moments when I wake up the next day, I consider not showing up to Bond's date at all. It would make things easier for me now, but harder in a couple days when I show up for our family sponsored "date". Or maybe he'll understand completely.

I should never have let him buy me a drink last night.

No. I really enjoyed his company, and I want to see him again. I don't care that we're rivals, or whether things will be weird when we officially meet. For once in my life, all I care about is the now.

And right now, I'm starving. I call up Sara. I know she's probably getting ready for her photo shoot, but who doesn't want to get some breakfast? She sounds sleepy when she answers, but agrees to meet me.

I throw on a pair of sweat pants and a tank top, put a light jacket over top, and go down to our favorite diner. It's just one building over from my apartment and it's where we like to talk about everything and nothing. I order us a couple cups of coffee before she arrives.

In a few minutes, a gorgeous blonde walks in. All eyes are

on her in those tight jeans and a tighter sweater, perfectly framing her generous hips and breasts. Even compared to me, she is a knockout.

She seems oblivious as she walks to the booth I'm sitting in, though I know she's anything but unaware. She makes a lot of money by flaunting those curves. She's a model and I know she'll make it big any day now.

"Hey there," she calls to me. I stand up and she gives me a hug.

"Good to see you," I say. We sit down. "Who's your client today?"

She rolls her eyes. "Another car dealership that wants a pretty blonde sitting on an expensive car for an ad. At least it's easy work."

I nod. Sara knows about my mob connections. She's a friend of the family, so to speak. She's gotten a couple of gigs because she knows the right people, but I try to keep her out of the darker parts of my life.

I want to talk to her about Bond, but I can't tell her exactly what's happening. Until things are certain and I have a ring on my finger, I can't really tell anyone about this. At least not all of it.

"So, you'll never believe this. I met a guy last night at the piano bar."

Sara's eyes light up. "Cara, you little minx! Tell me all about him."

The other patrons look over, but then look back at their newspapers and coffee. I grin at her and make a *Shh* sign. "What do you want to know?"

"Was he rich?"

Of course that would be the first question Sara would ask. "Yes, I think he was rich."

"Was he tall, dark, and handsome?"

I thought back to meeting Bond. He was at least six feet tall, definitely a good looking man, and those eyes were dark enough to steal my soul. I nod my head. "There's just one thing."

"There's always a catch."

"He's not a good dresser."

Sara laughs. "Deal breaker. You can have him. I won't steal him away from you."

I wanted to tell her more. I wanted to get an opinion of what I should do, but I don't want to put Sara at risk with information she shouldn't have.

"I'll need that in writing," I tease, changing my mind about telling her more.

"You got it. Let's order," Sara says. "I have to meet my client in three hours and I am not going on an empty stomach."

It's early December, but the tight jeans and sweater I pick out should keep me warm enough. Today is supposed to have sunshine. It looks quite a bit like Sara's outfit from earlier. I smile at the way the jeans and sweater hug my own curves. *Working with what Mama gave you*, I thought.

My thoughts flash back to my mom for a moment, and I quickly push the darkness that often follows from my mind. Today is all about fun, all about the now, and I shouldn't be thinking about the past at all. I take one last look in the mirror, wink at myself, then stroll out the door.

The piano bar never picks up until later in the evening, so it's practically deserted. However, there is one man sitting at the far side of the bar, nursing a drink.

For a moment, my breath is taken away again. Even from this distance, his dark brown eyes seem to pierce into my soul. He smiles, a wry, crooked smile that seems to show off just how handsome and confident he is.

He waves at me and I walk over to him. Again, his eyes wander up and down my body, making no move to disguise himself. It's an attractive quality, to be honest. He knows what he wants. As I get closer, I see he's wearing an expensive suit jacket and pants over a white, button up shirt. It's definitely nicer than what he was wearing last night.

"Hey there, Vesper" he says.

"Hey there, Bond," I reply. I wave my hand up and down his body. "I feel like I may have under-dressed for this. You're all dressed up now."

He chuckles. "It's all part of being a spy," he says. He gestures to the bar stool next to him, and I sit down. He orders me the same drink I was drinking yesterday.

"How was your day at work?" he asks.

"Work?" I say, forgetting that was my excuse for leaving so early last night. "Oh. Work. Stressful, but fine," I say, recovering quickly.

"Great. What did you say you do again?"

I draw in a deep breath. "I didn't," I say. I don't want to get caught in a lie, just in case he knows something about retail or whatever. I don't dare say anything about mattresses.

There's a pause between us. "Fair enough," he says when he finally figures out that I'm not talking.

"How about yourself?" I ask.

He makes a *tsk tsk* sound. "I'll tell you, if you tell me," he says.

My drink arrives. I raise my glass to cheers him and say, "I guess we're at an impasse, then."

He clinks my glass. "I'm usually better at negotiation than this."

I sip at my drink. "Maybe it's time to try a different negotiation strategy." I wonder just how many negotiation strategies he knows. Probably not all of them nice ones. That comes with being in the mafia.

He thinks about that for a moment. "My name's Dante," he says.

"That's not a very good negotiation tactic."

He shrugs his shoulders. "I guess I can keep calling you Vesper, then..."

He sounds like he's starting to give up the fight. I can throw him a bone here. "Lucia." I go with my middle name. That should be safe enough. "Or, at least that's what it says on my driver's license." As one of my names.

His eyes light up. "Lucia. That's good to know. And it's good to know that you have a driver's license."

I laugh. "So maybe I'm not as much of a rebel as I pretend to be. You, on the other hand, are still drinking in this bar."

"I told you, I own it," he says, this time much more matter-of-factly.

I roll my eyes. It's an act, because I do actually believe him. "Well then, Bond, should we spend the entire evening here so that you can get free drinks?"

He can't help but grin. "I had a better idea, Vesper. How often do you go to Central Park?"

"Never." Like most people who live in New York, I try to avoid the tourist traps.

"Then this should be a lot of fun."

Of course he has a limo waiting outside for us, one that I didn't even see him call. And of course he has a change of clothes in there.

The Russo Family likes to flaunt their status. They may be hurting for cash flow, but they won't let the rest of the world see that.

"Do you mind? I don't want to be overdressed for this date," he asks.

I laugh. "You want me to turn around?"

He shrugs. "Look out the window. I don't want you to get the wrong idea about me."

I can tell he's just teasing me, but I look out the window anyway. "Okay, I'm looking at some boring buildings instead of you."

"Good," he says. I can still see him in the reflection of the glass, and as he takes off his jacket and unbuttons his shirt. I like what I see. He's in great shape, with a set of muscular pecs and a six pack of abs. He throws on a soft t shirt and a light jacket over that. I try not to peek too much as he quickly slides into a pair of jeans. The fancy suit is tossed carelessly to the side. I wonder if he just came from a meeting.

"Okay, you can look now," he says.

I make an exaggerated look of surprise when I see his transformation. "That was quick."

He smiles. "I don't want to waste your time, Vesper."

I laugh. "So this is a date, now?"

"If you want it to be," he says with a shrug.

"Hey, your words, not mine," I say.

When the limo gets to Central Park, I let him help me out of the car. He immediately walks over to the closest hot dog stand and orders us two hot dogs. "Hope you don't mind, I'm starving."

My stomach is grumbling as well. It has been a long time since I had a street vendor hot dog. Most guys tended to take me to fancy restaurants on our dates.

We walk through Central Park, our hot dogs in hand. I'm still extremely surprised at how quickly I feel comfortable with him already. I never feel this way with anyone. I'm usually on edge, especially with anyone not from the family.

Yet, I feel comfortable around him. It's kind of exciting and wonderful.

"So, why the piano bar?" he asks.

I shrug. "I've always liked the piano. It seems like a sure-fire way of telling that someone is cultured."

"And that's what's important to you? Whether someone is cultured? I mean, I can play the piano and I don't feel too cultured," he says, that wry look back on his face.

"I don't know. I mean, when I play, I feel like a different person."

"You really do play? I thought you were just talking trash yesterday," he cuts in. I immediately regret saying anything.

"Well, yeah. I'm not all that good."

He shakes his head, as if he doesn't quite believe me. "I bet that's not true. I bet you practice every day. I bet you have a piano in your house."

I can feel my face immediately turn red. How could he have guessed that? "Joke's on you, I don't live in a house."

He looks at me. "Nobody in Manhattan lives in a house. You know what I meant."

I nodded softly. I did. "Well, somehow I believe that you live in a house."

He shrugs. "I used to. Not any more."

I leave it at that, and we continue to walk, eating our hot dogs. He turns us so that we are headed deep into the park. I wonder briefly if walking through Central Park with a rival crime mob member is a good idea, but I let him lead. I am safe with him. I trust him. I don't know why, but I feel like I would let him take me anywhere.

CHAPTER 5

When we arrive back at the piano bar after walking the park, he seems excited. It's not that he bounces around, but more that his movements have just a little more energy to them. He smiles more. There's a lightness in his step.

"Come on!" he says as he holds out his hand to help me out of the limo. He's smiling. It's contagious, and I can't help but laugh as he drags me toward the bar.

When we get inside, the place is filling up. Soft piano music plays from the speaker system instead of from the piano. They must be waiting for the piano player to arrive. However, when Dante enters the door and goes to the piano, the music cuts off. He starts playing some upbeat song and grabs the mic, something that he hadn't done all of yesterday.

"I want to thank all of you for coming out here tonight. I have a special guest joining me. Please welcome Vesper!"

My jaw drops in horror. He should have cleared this with me before putting me on the spot, but I don't think I can back down now. People are looking around and some have already fixated on the girl in the jeans and sweater.

The truth is, I've always wanted to play that piano. I just didn't think that it would happen like this.

I slowly start to walk toward the piano and people start to clap and whistle at me. Dante is such an asshole, I can't believe it. I'm a ball of nerves, both excited and apprehensive, and the whole time Dante just sits there with a big grin on his face. I feel like smacking him and kissing him all at the same time.

When I get to him, I cross my arms in front of me. He just looks up at me innocently and pats the spot on the bench next to him, beckoning me to sit down. I make an exaggerated sigh but sit next to him anyway.

"What do you know how to play?" he asks, putting his hand over the microphone.

"I can't play anything well," I tell him. Not compared to my mother.

He smiles at me. "Well, you better learn something quickly. A whole lot of people are expecting you to play."

I look around and see all eyes on me. For someone who helps run an entire organization, this feels strangely unnerving. Still, I manage to blink away all the people around me and just let my thoughts drive my body.

If I could chose to do anything, this is what I'd do every night. It's in my blood. My fingers begin to move across the keys, and I begin to play one of the classical pieces that I know by heart. Dante takes his hand off the mic and puts his fingers on the keys next to me.

I don't know if he has the backup music of this piece memorized, but he begins to play a note here and there that only seems to accentuate my own playing. It's similar to something my mother and I used to do as a game, but different enough that I don't compare him to my mother. I do know that it takes a talented musician to play like this on the fly, and the synergy I feel with him as my fingers slowly play the notes just brings me closer to him.

I lose track of time as I continue to play, shifting from one piece to the next, Dante by my side the entire time. I can feel the heat of his body radiating into mine. His leg presses against me and I can smell the clean scent of his soap. I like the way he feels next to me.

We play for what seems like hours. It's effortless to play with him. It's like we share a mind and every note we play sounds better when we play it together. I didn't know it was possible to have a connection with another person through a piano like that. There are some in the bar who have gone back to milling around or drinking with friends, but we have built up a pretty sizable audience. When I stop playing, they burst into applause. I love the sound.

When I stand up, Dante grabs my arm. He grabs the mic and says "Can we give an extra round of applause to Vesper?" The entire bar looks our way and begins to clap. No matter how many times a man has told me how beautiful I am, I've never felt as beautiful and sexy as I did in that moment.

Dante smiles and takes my hand, leading me over to the bar. Two drinks are waiting for us, and he hands me one of them.

"So," I start. "How often do you put ladies on the spot like that?"

He shrugs. "That's the first time that I did it to someone else, but a friend of mine once put me on the spot like that when I was learning to play the guitar."

I smile when I think of him being as uncomfortable as I was just a moment ago. "Well, thank you. I always wanted to play piano in this bar some day, so I guess I just got my wish earlier than I thought."

He's all smiles, and it seems like he can't stop looking at me. Suddenly, he leans forward, tilts my chin up with his finger, and kisses me. It takes me by surprise, and for a moment, he seems like he might pull back. Then, he doubles down and presses into me further. I kiss back, feeling his muscular chest and abs against me. The heat between us is incredible. We are incredible.

I break from the kiss. There are several onlookers, same as when I had played the piano, though I don't feel like putting this kind of show on for them. I do, however, want to continue to play this music with him.

"I have a piano in my apartment, Bond. What do you think about going up to my apartment to play for a smaller audience?" I ask.

He has a wry grin on. "I would like that very much, Vesper."

As we ride the elevator up to my apartment, I can tell that he wants to take me right there in the elevator so badly, and that something is holding him back. His eyes look at me hungrily, as if I'm the prize he has been waiting for all week.

Again, I wonder if he knows who I am. He hasn't said anything, so I assume he thinks I'm just a regular girl. I don't know why, but it makes me feel a little bit guilty.

When I open the door to my apartment, he pushes me into the wall and begins to kiss me. Suddenly, he breaks away. I practically whimper as he pulls away. "I don't believe it," he says.

"What?" I ask. I quickly scan my apartment, wondering if I left out something that easily identifies me as a member of the Savio Family.

He gestures toward the corner of the room. "You actually do have a piano up here. I thought that was just a line."

I laugh. He pulls off his jacket, tossing it on the back of

the couch, and practically skips over to the piano and sits down, starting to play. It's one of the pieces that he played the night before, obviously one of his favorites. I cross the room and stand next to the piano, crossing my arms and frowning.

He notices me after a moment and ends the piece in an exaggerated manner. "Of course, where are my manners? I didn't come here to play this instrument." Showing exactly what he did come up to play, he stands up and moves to me, moving his hands to my hips and lifting me up. He kisses me hungrily as I wrap my legs around him, locking my feet behind his muscular ass. My fingers go behind his strong shoulders, wrapping around his body.

He begins to walk, bringing us toward the bedroom as his hands firmly grab my ass. Before we get there I pull his shirt up over his head. His hair, which was just the right amount of messed up before, is now even more messy. I run my hand through his hair, trying to smooth it back out, but its no use. He seems to be oblivious to it as he leans back in to kiss me.

When we get to the bed, he throws me down on it. I'm glad I didn't leave a stiletto or something in there. For a moment he stands over me, clearly thinking about what he'd like to do to me. He undoes the belt of his slacks, pushing them down to the ground. I smile as I'm finally able to see how hard he had already gotten through his boxers. I unbutton my jeans and begin to push them down but he stops me.

His lips meet the top of my panties and begin to kiss downward. I gasp for a moment as he puts pressure on my clit through my underwear, but instead of lingering, he keeps moving down. He begins to pull on my jeans, and I arch my hips to allow him to pull them off. He kisses his way down my leg as he pulls, sending shivers down my spine.

As he begins to kiss back up my legs, I pull off my

sweater. The white bra and panties that I'd picked that day was nothing special, I didn't plan for things to go this far. Still, he looks at me ravenously, as if I am dressed in the most provocative outfit I own.

He lowers himself over my body, kissing me fiercely. He has an energy that I rarely feel in men, and I enjoy it. He seems to match every movement, every writhe my body makes.

"Lie down on the bed," I say. I stand up and kiss him, placing my hands on his shoulders and guiding him down. He smiles as I reach behind me and unclasp my bra, allowing my breasts to be exposed to the world. I run my fingers up the sides of his legs, up underneath the fabric of his boxers. I bunch the fabric up, grabbing them in handfuls, and begin to pull them down.

He audibly groans as his cock is set free, springing from his pants. His V-shaped groin muscles point down in the most delectable way. I immediately trace the V lines down with my fingers, feeling the muscles attached, wondering how good it's going to feel to have those muscles thrusting into me.

I move my hand to grasp the base of his shaft, then lick from the bottom to the head in one smooth, long lick. He watches me with a smile on his face as I envelop the head with my mouth, looking up at him sweetly.

"You are so beautiful, Lucia," he says to me. Reverence fills his voice.

I'm not used to people saying my name like that, even if it's not really my name. It makes me feel warm and tingly inside. I reach for a condom in my nightstand and quickly slide it onto him. I smile and crawl my way up to kiss him. I feel him at my entrance, hard and ready, and I let myself slide over him. He gasps as he enters me, and I gasp as well, surprised at how good he feels inside of me.

I begin to writhe against him, moaning into our kiss as we move together. His hands go to my ass, moving me up and down as he begins to thrust into me, going even deeper than he had before. I gasp and throw myself up, kneeling over him as he continues to thrust. His hands go to my tits, kneading them and pinching at my nipples. As he leans up to a sitting position to kiss them, I rub my hands all through his hair.

His hands grasp my back tightly, pulling me in farther as we begin to move in tandem. Our every motion is reflected onto the other, and I feel a synergy that I've never felt with a man before. We are perfectly matched. It's like we are made for one another. I think he feels it, too, because he begins to make grunts that are just so hot. I thought that because of his youth, I would be showing him how to do things, but he knows what to do almost better than I do.

Suddenly, he lifts me up, then rolls over with me on the bottom. I come crashing down to the bed with him still inside of me, and he barely misses a beat. He's thrusting into me, and I get to watch that ass as he fills me over and over again. As he pistons into me, his dick rubs against my clit in just the right way, and I find myself getting closer and closer to orgasm. I haven't felt this level of pleasure in ages. It's hard and fast and exactly what we both need.

"Lucia, Lucia..." I love the way he pants my name.

"Yes," I gasp, wanting this more than I've ever wanted anything in my life.

He groans, his body going deep into mine. I can feel the bliss radiating through him as he loses himself to me.

We lay there for a while after that. My breathing takes a while to slow down, while Dante seems to catch his almost immediately. He lays there, looking at me, rubbing his fingers up and down my body. I smile at him while tracing the lines of his muscles gently.

"I have to go," he says after a long time. "I don't want to, but I do."

I sigh. We never should have done this in the first place. He doesn't know who I really am. I feel a little guilty, but I'm still high on an orgasm, so I don't really feel as guilty as I should.

"Can I see you again?" I ask, watching him as he stands up and starts to pull his boxers back up.

"Tomorrow?" he asks.

I frown. "I have to work. It's important. Maybe the next day?"

We are supposed to meet in two days. I have this quick fantasy of telling him that I'm actually his new fiancee at our family sponsored date. He'd smile and laugh. We'd have a wonderful time.

I hope that's how it goes. I can also see him getting angry at my deception. I know I would be upset if we were reversed.

His brow darkens. He runs his hand through his dark hair and looks up at the ceiling.

"Sorry, I can't. I have to meet someone for my family."

"That doesn't sound bad," I say.

His shoulders slump. "I hate to tell you this, but it's the woman my parents want me to marry. I should have told you, but..." He shrugs. "I wanted you."

It's funny hearing him say that but I like knowing that he wants me.

"You didn't make me any promises. Do you know what she looks like at least?" I ask, trying to sound innocent. I was shown his picture. Did he not see mine?

"Did you know that veils were used so that a groom wouldn't see how ugly his new arranged marriage bride was until it was too late?" He shrugs. "It's kind of like that. It's better for me not to know."

He's afraid that I'm going to be ugly. A part of me smiles. He's in for a nice surprise.

"Maybe she'll be the girl of your dreams," I tell him.

He shrugs and pulls on his shirt. I'm sad to see his bare skin disappear. He looks over at me, a sadness in his dark eyes.

"I doubt it." He leans forward and kisses my forehead.

"Well, you know where I live now," I tell him. "Maybe you can come see me again if she doesn't work out."

He doesn't smile as he looks away. He puts on his pants.

"I had a really great time with you tonight," he says, looking over at me. He stands up. "Thanks for tonight."

He kisses my forehead one last time and then leaves my apartment.

I stare after him, still laying naked in my bed. He thinks he's going to have to marry someone terrible. I'm actually sort of looking forward to officially meeting him now.

CHAPTER 6

"It has been a pleasure seeing you again, Chief O'Brien," I say with a smile. I'm standing in a fancy hotel ballroom surrounded by powerful people. I wear a dark blue dress that makes me look like I belong here. I look like a socialite.

Today, is a local fundraiser for the police force. A fancy dinner at a hotel with a silent auction afterwards with the intent to raise money. I'm here representing the Savio Mattress Company.

They certainly raised a lot of Savio money today, I think to myself with a smile.

"I'm so glad we still have such a good working relationship," the man I'm talking to replies. He's in his late sixties, but still looking trim and handsome in his official police uniform. His wife wears diamond earrings that a woman married to a man in the public sector shouldn't be able to afford.

I know that my money paid for those, too.

"It's important for local businesses to have ties to the community," I respond with a practiced smile. "I'm so glad that you are willing to work with my family. For the betterment of the community, of course."

The police chief smiles. This is all a game and we both know it. My family has been paying him for a long time. The police never bother our business operations. It's a good deal for both of us.

"Tell your aunt and uncle hello for me, won't you?" the police chief asks. "Although, I must say, it is wonderful having you here. You're much prettier in a dress than your uncle."

I chuckle. "I'll make sure to tell him that."

This is a part of the business that I'm actually very good at. I've slowly been taking over the business. My aunt and uncle want to retire eventually, so they've slowly been training me on things. This year, I've been responsible for all the official meetings. As far as it looks to the outside, I'm simply taking up all the social engagements. However, a lot of business is done at the local events.

Not all of the meetings the mob does are in back alleys or dark offices. Many of them are out in broad daylight. We meet at restaurants and attend social functions. There's no better way to make a company look legitimate than to do legitimate things.

Today, I made sure that the police are still in my pocket. They don't mind us much since we keep to ourselves for the most part. Since we aren't slinging drugs or selling off children, we are a lower threat. Throw some generous "donations" in, and the police force is happy to turn a blind eye to the less-than legal side of my family business.

"Have you met Senator Grayson?" He asks me, motioning to a man coming our direction.

I shake my head no.

"Let me introduce you." He waves hello to the incoming

senator. "Senator, this is Cara Savio. She runs Savio Mattresses."

The senator shakes my hand. His hand is firm and strong. He's an older man as most politicians are, with silver hair and pale blue eyes. I'm always wary of men called senator, and even though he looks nice enough, I won't trust him farther than I can throw him.

"It's very nice to meet you, Senator." I smile.

"It's very nice to meet you," he says to me. "Your mother was Caroline Jeffries, right? I once had the privilege of hearing your mother play once. It's stayed with me all these years. She was extraordinary."

My eyes widen slightly. Not many people put my mother's married name with the Savio family. "Thank you."

"I was actually hoping to meet you here," he says. "The police chief has spoken very highly of you."

My surprise at him knowing my mother diminishes slightly. He did his research on me. I wonder if he really did hear my mother play. It's cynical, but I've had enough experience with politicians not to be stupid.

"I didn't have an interest in supporting politicians that help my family's business," I tell him.

He smiles, but it's a business smile. "I think our interests definitely align in that regard."

"Are you running for re-election?"

He nods. "I'm favored to keep the seat, but I still need every advantage I can get."

"I'll be sure to contribute to your campaign fund," I promise.

It's always good to have a senator in your pocket. It never hurts to have friends in high places. We have enough funds that a donation to buy some good will is a smart plan.

"Thank you very much," he says with a sincere smile. At

least it passes as sincere. "Your mother played in Michigan. I believe she was involved with senator Norwood at the time?"

My chest tightens slightly, the way it always does when someone speaks of Senator Norwood.

"Yes." I don't elaborate.

"Are you supporting his campaign as well?"

"Hell no." It comes out stronger than I mean to.

The senator looks surprised. "You don't like him?"

"He was the last person to see my mother alive, and I'm still not convinced there wasn't foul play around her death," I say diplomatically. It's not wise to accuse a powerful politician of murder at a private function full of politicians. "I'm not his biggest fan."

He nods. "My protege is running against him this election." He leaves the rest open.

"I would be incredibly interested in donating to that campaign," I quickly tell him. "I would love nothing better than to see him lose."

The senator gives me a predatory smile. "I'll be sure to get you his information," he says. "I have to say, senator Norwood is not my favorite person either. I'm not sure how scandal hasn't taken him down yet."

"He has a lot of money and money buys loyalty," I tell him. That's true for my business as well.

"Yes, but it only buys it for a time. Bought loyalty is different than shared interest," Senator Grayson replies. "I believe you and I have a shared interest."

Senator Grayson would make a great mobster. But, then the qualities that make a good mob boss would also prove useful in politics.

"Why don't you like the senator?" I ask, giving him a coy smile. I doubt the senator killed his mother.

"He's not only a rival, he's a scum-ball," the senator

replies. "I've seen the things he gets away with and I don't approve. He gives politicians a bad name."

I raise my eyebrows slightly. I wonder if the senator is just trying to impress me or if he really does think Norwood is slime. Either way, I feel like we're on the same team, which was what he was going for.

"Please make sure I get the information for your race and your protege," I tell him.

"I'll be sure to do that," he replies. "It really was a pleasure meeting you, Cara."

"Likewise."

"And just so you don't think that I'm just trying to get on your good side, I saw your mother perform Clair de Lune on September eighteenth. She wore a dark blue dress not too different than the one you're wearing now. I still remember it because it was the most beautiful thing I've ever heard."

It hits me like a punch to the gut. That was a real performance. He really did hear my mother play.

Suddenly, I just want to go home. I don't want to smile and be polite to men only interested in me for my money and what I can give them.

I thank the senator and quickly make my goodbyes to go home.

CHAPTER 7

I hurry home. I'm a ball of emotions. Thoughts of my mother and Senator Norwood run through my head. I've tried to avoid anything to do with Norwood. He knows who I am. He tried to get custody of me after my mother died, but luckily she had a will that made it so I went with my aunt and uncle.

I sometimes have nightmares of what would have happened to me if I'd lived with him instead. I probably wouldn't be alive.

I need to eat. Food always makes me feel better. I call Sara, wanting to see her. She always knows how to make me feel better.

"Hello?" I hear a groggy voice on the other end of the phone.

"Sara? Are you okay?" I ask.

"Yeah, yeah, just a little hungover. What's up?"

It isn't like Sara to drink with a client, even on a Saturday night. "Well, I got a crazy story to tell about Delgado, but it sounds like you've got a story to tell also. Want some pie?"

I'm not really hungry, but I want the company.

"Yeah, I could use some food."

Just like the other day, I beat Sara down to the diner. This time, however, she doesn't make a grand entrance. An average looking girl wearing a pair of sweat pants and pajama top opens the door to the diner. Not a single head turns as she makes her way over to me.

"You look awful," I say with a disarming smile.

"Yeah, well..." she says, trailing off. As she slumps into the chair across from me, she seems kind of out of it.

"Hey, are you okay?" I ask. She looks a little green around the edges and her hair and skin are dull.

"I feel better today, but Friday... I spent yesterday recovering. I had a little too much to drink trying to forget."

"Why's that?"

She shudders a little, as if she doesn't want to remember the details. "I got a call from a photographer, night before last. Some girl got sick and had to cancel on him, so he was desperate. The amount he offered was more than I usually get for a modeling gig, so I took it."

"Doesn't sound so bad," I say. Sara often did modeling work not through her agency. It was an easy way to get some extra money on free nights.

She laughs, but it's a hollow laugh. "Not yet. I thought the extra money was just because it was last minute. It was an escort job. And not the willing kind."

"Are you okay?" I ask, worried.

"I called Ethan when things got rough. He rescued me." She wraps her arms around herself. "He was the only person I could think of."

"What part of town where you in?" I ask, thinking of my family business. We don't condone this kind of thing.

"North. On the edge of Savio territory. That's why I thought I was safe." Sara sniffles.

North is Russo territory.

This isn't good for our two families. We are trying to make an alliance, but I won't join with people who force women into sex.

"I'll get to the bottom of this," I tell Sara.

Sara looks at me with big, scared eyes. The Russos let this happen. I've been thinking all this time of just the normal repercussions of marriage. I haven't stop to consider the political ramifications. There are things that need to be discussed.

If this is business as usual, then I don't know if I can marry him.

"Let's get some food in you," I say. I know I think better on a full stomach.

Sara nods. We both stare at our menus, not really looking at the food options. I need to find out exactly what the Russos are doing before I sign on the dotted line.

My mind is going a million miles per minute. I can't seem to focus for more than a couple of seconds on anything. Too much anger. Too much anxiety. Too much responsibility.

I sit down at the piano and start to play. As I begin to play the song, I think of how great it sounds. *Stick with the plan,* the voice in my head says, *and everything will turn out just fine.*

Then I think of how much better it sounded when Dante was sitting there in the piano bar, playing just a few notes that intersected with mine. I think of when we made love, how our bodies seemed to play off of one another to make beautiful music.

It doesn't match with Sara's experience.

For now, I decide to just wait. When I see him again, I can decide what my feelings actually are. I don't have to decide right this second. I can just live in the moment for a little while and see where things take me. I'll see him soon enough. I'm just meeting him tomorrow. It's not like the wedding is planned yet.

When my intercom buzzes, I think about not answering it, but only for a moment. Almost no one knows where I live. It's probably just a lost visitor for someone else. I sigh and press the button.

"Hello?"

"Vesper."

Dante's voice sends warm shivers down my spine. I'm suddenly giddy at seeing him again. It's at complete odds with what I was just feeling, but I don't care. "Come up."

I buzz him in, and find myself nervous the entire time that he's on his way up.

He shows up at my door looking like a rebel without a cause. Leather jacket, sexy jeans, and a windblown look to his hair that screams that he just doesn't care.

My breath catches in my lungs for a moment, but I recover quickly. "What are you doing here?"

"I wanted to see you. It's stupid, but..." He shrugs.

My whole body warms as I smile.

"Want to go for a ride?" he asks.

I frown, not understanding.

"Motorcycle."

It's December and there is no way I'm getting on the back of motorcycle without a helmet with the head of a rival crime lord. That has bad idea written all over it.

"I'll make you a deal, Bond. When you get two helmets, I'll ride with you."

He smiles. "Deal. So, I did intend to bring you to my favorite diner, but..."

"But we would need to travel there by bike," I finish for him.

He taps his nose with his finger. "I do know of a great New York pizza place."

I smile. "If you're buying, I'm in."

The pizzeria is exactly where I expect a teenager to hang out, not a mobster. Still, some of my favorite first dates had been in places just like this. "Is there anything you don't like?" he asks me.

I shake my head. When you have a job like mine, you learn to like a wide variety of foods and activities that you never thought you would.

That seems to make him happy. "One with everything on it," he says, then grabs a soda from the counter. We head to a booth.

There's not even an ingredient list on the wall, so it's a real mystery to me what we're getting. "What all is 'everything'?" I ask.

Dante smiles and shakes his head. "You'll see." I can tell he's enjoying my apprehension.

I decide to test him out. I want to know how he's going to react tomorrow when we officially meet. "Do you like surprises, Bond?"

He looks away from me. "Yeah, sure. I mean nothing really surprises me that much."

"Oh yeah, Mr. Tough Guy. I'm sure you just expected to talk me into sleeping with you the other night."

He smiles, looks away again, and shrugs. It's the perfect level of cockiness and just manages to turn me on even more. I slap his arm and he leans over and kisses me. A few moments later I laugh as I realize I'm making out in a pizzeria like a teenager again. If nothing else, Bond will keep me young.

We keep kissing until the guy at the counter calls Dante's name. He jumps out of the booth and grabs the pizza, setting it down in front of me. It's a steaming mess of what seems like a thousand different ingredients.

If nothing else, he's definitely a sadist, I think to myself as I look at the melange of difference meats and vegetables on the pie in front of me. So when I grab a slice out and bite into it, I'm not surprised that his eyes look at me like I did the exact opposite of what he expected.

The taste isn't the worst I've ever had. At least it's all-American. However, I probably won't be able to finish the whole slice. Still, I chew it up and swallow. "Surprised, Bond?" I ask with a smile.

He smiles back. "I do like some surprises," he says. He digs into the pizza, obviously not one to be outdone. We smile back and forth as we eat, just making small talk. I suspect that we both know that neither one of us is telling the whole truth.

As we walk back to my apartment, we go slow. He puts his jacket on me which warms me against the cold December air. I enjoy his arm around me, and he feels strong underneath me. Still, I can tell what he's going to be angling for already, and I'm not entirely sure if I want that or not.

When we get to the door of my apartment, we both step inside the outer door. "So..." he starts.

"So."

There's a pause, then he smiles and laughs. "Are you going to invite me up?"

I think of Sara and what happened to her on his turf. Anger flares up in my stomach.

I smile at him. "I don't know. After the gross pizza we just ate, I'm not sure I should."

He makes an exaggerated pout. "I'll make sure to get you a cheese pizza just for you next time."

I laugh, but don't respond to the pizza comment.

"I get it, I get it. Thursday night was a one time thing." He says it so nonchalantly that it makes my chest ache.

"That's not it, I just... I just don't know if we should do this again so fast."

That, and I won't want to stop. If he comes in, I'm likely to say something I shouldn't. I'll say something about what happened to Sara. I'll mess up the partnership my aunt and uncle have worked so hard on. I don't want to screw this marriage plan up because I couldn't keep my temper under control.

I look up at him and nearly give in. Those dark eyes draw me in. There's danger in them, but they're dark and warm. "I don't know if I'll get to see you again."

Damn. He's really trying hard to break down my defenses. It takes all the effort I can muster to stop mooning over him and turn toward the inner door to my apartment building. For a moment after I turn my back to him and put the key in the lock, I have the terrifying thought that he'll try to force his way in. He does nothing of the sort, of course, and I feel silly for thinking it.

"Good night, Bond."

"Good nigh, Vesper."

I close the door to my apartment and immediately regret turning Dante away. As far as he knows, he's going to meet some bimbo tomorrow and he'll never see me again. Or, he'll have to cheat to see me. I appreciate that he thinks he isn't going to cheat. He seems to feel that this marriage thing is pretty final.

"Just one more day," I whisper to myself. Then I'll be able to think clearly again.

CHAPTER 8

I wear a white dress. That seems like the color I should wear to meet my future husband. It's short enough to be flirty, but still long enough that my aunt won't give me the evil eye. It's classy. I combine it with white pumps and I make sure my hair and makeup look amazing.

Now that it's time to officially meet him, I'm nervous. Ethan says that the men who assaulted Sara were definitely Russo's.

It makes me wonder who I'm getting into bed with.

Not to mention that he's not expecting me. He's expecting a stranger. Someone who doesn't play piano. It should be a good surprise, but not everyone reacts well to surprises.

We stopped throwing surprise parties for my grandfather after he pulled out his Glock and shot the balloons. I just hope that Dante takes surprises without a gun.

Ethan picks me up outside my apartment. He tells me he hasn't heard anything new about Sara. He tells me that I better behave myself. Aunt Sophia and Uncle Tony have a lot riding on this. This meeting isn't about me. It's about the Savios and the Russos.

I know he's just looking out for me and the family, but I can't think of anything other than Dante.

I'm supposed to meet Dante in the lobby of a hotel. We're supposed to then go to dinner with the families. I'm shocked that both sides agreed to let us meet on our own. I suppose it does make things a little more romantic. At least we won't have our families breathing down our necks.

I'm so nervous at this point, I'm afraid I'm going to throw up.

When the limo pulls up, I can already see Dante in the lobby, leaning against a pillar. He's wearing a sexy suit, obviously dressed to impress. He is about to meet his future wife.

Ethan opens the limo door, and I step out. Dante sees me get out of the limo and I see him smile. For a moment, I think that everything is going to be okay, that maybe he knew who I was all along, that maybe he just doesn't care. I let relief wash through me.

I begin to walk up to him, a smile on my face. He takes a second look at my body and face, and then a third. Confusion fills his face.

I step right up to him. "Hello, Mr. Russo."

"You can't be here right now," he tells me. "You need to leave."

I shrug, not knowing what to say. My stomach has stopped twisting and is now just a pit of ice. I'm not sure if it's an improvement or not. "My name isn't really Lucia. It's Cara. Cara Lucia Savio."

His eyes go wide. "Who put you up to this? I told Frank about you. Did he put you up to this? This isn't funny."

"No, no joke. I'm Cara Savio of the Savio Family."

He blinks twice and then turns and walks away.

CHAPTER 9

He doesn't look back as he walks out of the hotel. I can see him pause as he sees Ethan in his limo, the final confirmation that this isn't an elaborate prank. He looks back at me with teenage anger in his eyes. I have betrayed him and he hates me for it. Then he heads down the block, walking with an enraged energy away from the hotel.

Ethan gets out of the limo. "Mr. Russo!" he calls after Dante. Dante doesn't even look back. He doesn't even pause. Ethan looks over at me, a question on his lips. He takes one last look down the street, but I can't see Dante anymore and I doubt Ethan will be able to much longer.

My brave face crumbles and my knees buckle. Ethan rushes over to me and practically has to catch me to keep me from falling on the floor. Everything is ruined. I'm struggling to breathe, to find the will to live. I haven't felt this way in a decade. Not since...

I push that thought out of my mind. Ethan wraps his arms around me, steadying me. "What happened?" he asked. His gruff voice is gentle. He doesn't know that this is all my fault.

I shake my head, unable to talk for the moment and unwilling to tell him anyway. Ethan holds me for a moment, waiting for me to answer, but then seems to notice all the eyes on us. "Come on, I'll help you to the car."

I stagger to the limo. *I must look terrible,* I think to myself. My makeup is smeared around my eyes, and my legs still shaky underneath me. *We'll be lucky if hotel security doesn't stop us on the way out.*

Nobody questions us, and Ethan opens the door for me, allowing me to collapse into the car. Ethan quickly runs around to the driver door, letting himself in and driving us away.

"Now, you're going to tell me exactly what just happened," he says, his voice full of authority. I can see his eyes in the rear-view mirror and I look away. I know I shouldn't defy him at this point, but I can't help it.

"Just take me home," I plead, burying my face into the seat cushion.

I hear a long, exaggerated sigh. Then the locks click. "I'm driving you home, but you're not leaving this car until you tell me what just happened."

The car starts to move and I sob against the seat, unaware of how much time is passing. All I know is that what might have been my one chance at love is gone, gone because of this job. I had something wonderful, but it was based on a lie. It's my life on repeat yet again.

Soon, I'm aware that the car has stopped near my apartment building. The engine is still on but we're not moving. Ethan is giving me a moment. I look up and he's looking at me. "I was serious, Cara. I have to tell Miss White something."

I open my mouth to talk, then close it quickly. "I can't," I say.

"You can and you will, or else I'll drive you to Aunt

Sophia's home right now. Trust me when I say you don't want that."

I know I don't want that. That's the last thing in the world I want. I've failed my family.

I curl into a miserable ball in the back seat. I don't want to move. The shame of how much I just screwed up is overwhelming.

"Stay in the car," Ethan says. I hear the car door open.

I listen for the driver's side door to shut, but it doesn't. Instead, I hear voices.

"Mr. Russo. I didn't expect to see you here."

There's a pause. My heart is racing like a scared rabbit's. What is he doing here?

"I don't think we've officially met. Can I see Cara?" There's a pause and I can only imagine what Ethan is thinking about Dante. Dante's voice is all confidence as he asks, "Is there a problem?"

"No, no problem at all." Ethan takes his time opening the door. I see his eyes as he leans in and whispers, "Get out. You can still save this."

I compose myself quickly, wiping my hands under my eyes to try and remove some of the mascara runoff. I know my tears have mostly ruined my makeup, but there's nothing I can do about that now. I get out of the limo with practiced grace and see Dante, looking a little sheepish. His expression seems to melt a bit as he sees what a mess I am.

"You can tell me how he knows where you live later," Ethan whispers to me as he helps me out of the limo. In a much louder voice he says, "Have a good evening, Mr. Russo."

"Thank you," Dante replies, his eyes never leaving me. He extends an arm and I eagerly wrap my own arm around it. It feels so warm in the cold December air and just touching him makes me feel better. Hope that things are going to work out is starting to bubble in my stomach, though I do my best to keep it down. I take one last look back before we enter the doors of my building to see Ethan. He's watching us, arms crossed and face stony.

The two of us go up the elevator in silence. I can tell Dante wants to say something, but I can wait. I secretly dread what he has to say but at this point, I don't even care as long as he's with me. It's almost sick how happy I am to have him here right now. I have no idea what he is going to say, or do, but I don't care. Right now, he's not walking away from me anymore.

I open the door to my apartment and he walks in. I turn to shut the door behind me and when I turn back he has me pressed up against it. With terrible slowness, he leans forward and kisses me. I immediately melt into him, my body realizing what it almost lost. I drink him in, relishing every taste. We kiss for what seems like minutes before he pulls his mouth away from mine. "Sit down for a minute," he says.

My smile fades. I know that the moment we just had wasn't necessarily a sign that he forgave me, but I hope he has anyway. I quickly walk over to the piano, taking a seat at the piano bench. He follows, then stops and crosses his arms with out sitting.

"I'm sorry I reacted the way I did at the hotel," he says after a moment. "I thought it was a prank. I told my brother Frank that I'd met someone that had me reconsidering marrying the Savio family. It would be like him to put you there just to watch me squirm."

"I should have told you," I tell him. "I just didn't know how. It wasn't fair to surprise you."

"It would have been a nice surprise if I hadn't told Frank," Dante admits with a small smile." I've never met a woman like you. You make me feel things..."

His words take my breath away. I can hardly speak, but I manage to whisper, "I've never met a man like you either."

Dante puts one knee on the ground, taking my hands in his.

"So, you want to get married?" he asks me. "I don't have the ring on me now, unfortunately."

I don't let him finish the sentence, I just lean in and kiss him. He isn't expecting it and he topples backward, hitting the floor. "Are you okay?" I ask quickly. Nothing is going right tonight.

He easily gets back up on his knees, putting his head below mine and looking up at me. "Better than okay," he says, and I giggle. I'm still crying, but it's more that I can't stop than anything else. His hands go to my sides, feeling me through the dress as he tips his face up to kiss me. "So I take it this is a *'yes'*?"

I nod. "Yes."

His grin lights up the room. With that, his fingers begin to hike up my dress and his hands caress my inner thighs. I'm so happy that I can't help but melt into him for another kiss. "Will you help me out of my dress?"

His dark eyes sparkle as I stand up. I kick off my shoes, then turn around. I can feel him standing, at least a full head taller than me, as he fumbles a little with the hook and latch that keeps my dress pulled together. When he finally gets it, he takes his time unzipping me, obviously savoring the sight of the bare skin of my back. It falls to the floor and I step out of it, turning around to let him see. His eyes scan me up and down. I've never much liked it when a man looks at me like I'm a piece of meat, but when Dante does it, I love it. When he does it, I feel beautiful not bought.

I step toward him, clad in nothing but my bra, panties, and stockings. "I think you're wearing too many clothes," I say, slowly dropping to my knees. I undo his belt, looking up at him while I do it. He pulls off his shirt and lets it fall to the floor behind him. I bite my lip at the sight of his smooth, muscled chest. It's a girl's wet dream. I unbutton his pants, and when I begin to pull down on his zipper, I notice how rock hard he is. I smile.

When I finally get his cock out, I don't even hesitate, I just begin by sticking my tongue out and licking from the base of his shaft all the way to the tip. He audibly groans, making me smile as I take him into my mouth. I begin to swirl his head around the front of my mouth, going shallow. Then suddenly, I take him as deep as I can. His fingers tangle in my hair and his whole body tightens at the sudden rush of pleasure. I relish the sound of him gasping as I begin to suck on him.

After a few moments he moves his hands, running his fingers through my hair. The feeling of his touch drives me wild, and I increase my efforts, getting his dick as wet as I can.

He pulls me to my feet and leans down to give me a kiss. I leap up and wrap my legs around him. His hands palm my ass as he begins to walk toward the bedroom. His huge rod is rubbing up against my black panties, and I can't wait to feel him inside of me.

I don't want to wait the ten steps to get to the bed. I pull my panties to the side, allowing him to enter me. He pauses for a moment at my entrance, and our eyes meet. His eyes are deep water and the world swims in them. I shift my hips and I'm so ready that he slides in as if he was always supposed to be a part of me. Raw desire catches in my throat as he penetrates me, and I moan loudly, surprised at just how turned on I am.

I grind up against him and he massages his fingers into my ass cheeks, taking full advantage of this situation. My pulse is racing with sheer want and pleasure. When we get to the bed he pauses, but I keep bouncing up and down on him, feeling him fill every inch of me. He holds my body up as if I am weightless. As he lowers us both to the bed, he nearly leaves me, but I arch my hips to keep him inside of me. It's shallow, but he stays with me. As soon as my back is on the bed, he thrusts himself to the hilt, somehow filling me even fuller than I had ever thought possible.

His arms wrap around me as his hips begin to piston into me. I pull him to me, trying to draw him in even further. I can tell he's going crazy with lust, plowing into me with reckless abandon. If I let him continue, he'll finish now and I'm not ready for that.

I push him off of me and stand up. "Lay on the bed," I command. He does so without hesitating, never taking his eyes off of me. I pull down my panties and stockings at the same time, then unhook my bra and let it fall to the floor. He looks at me like a starving man in a buffet. I bend over and kiss up his leg, giving his cock another lick from the base to the tip of his shaft again. I hear him mutter to himself, as if he can hardly believe what's going on. I climb onto the bed and straddle him, feeling his hardness between my legs. His eyes glow with want and I gladly take him inside me again.

His hands grab my hips as I bounce up and down on him. He fixates on my chest, so I squeeze my arms together to make my breasts look bigger as I work his body up and down. His pupils go wide and he licks his lips, thrusting up even harder. I whimper with how good it feels and his hands work their way up my back, pulling me down so that our bodies make contact. He jackhammers into me, giving me everything he's got.

I can tell that he is going to come soon, so I whisper in his ear to spur him on. "Oh yeah, baby. Come in me. I want you to come in me, baby."

I know that no man can resist that invitation, and within

a few moments I can feel him swelling. My own body reacts, pushing onward to take his every inch. I moan softly in his ear, giving him exactly what I know he wants. His hands grasp for purchase on my back, finally settling on my ass and squeezing.

He spreads me open, and in a moment I feel his seed filling my body. He shudders as he shoots, losing his body to me. Gasping, I contract on him, my body flying high on combined pleasure and milking him for all he has. My eyes roll back into my head as he continues to pound into me. I lose my mind to the sensation of his body completing me in a way no one has for years.

For a few moments he keeps thrusting, then he slows to a stop. He relaxes his death grip on my ass and flexes his fingers to resume blood flow. I arch my back, still high on the drug that is Dante Russo.

I kiss the tip of his nose and he smiles at me.

I roll over and stand up, careful not to make a mess on my sheets. He's splayed out on my bed, all muscles and hard lines. I'm tempted to run my tongue along some of them. "I have to go to the bathroom really quick. Don't go anywhere, though."

"I'm not going anywhere," he says with a smile. I return the smile and go to the bathroom to clean up.

When I come back out, he's standing at the window. I admire his ass for a moment, perfectly sculpted against the light of the New York skyline. I still want my snuggles, so I know I have to lure him back to the bed.

As I come up behind him, he says, "You have a great view here."

I shrug and wrap my arms around his waist. I love the way his muscles tighten at my touch. I look out the window at the lights and pause. It's been a long time since I've actually taken the time to look out the window.

"There's too much light pollution here. I can't see any stars from here."

Dante tilts his head. "I hardly notice the lack of stars, but then again you must not be from New York."

"Not originally," I reply. I think of my mother and find that I'm sad. She would have liked Dante. He's not the type of man she would have picked for me, but then this life isn't the one she wanted for me either.

He watches me for a moment, waiting for me to tell him more about myself. I don't like talking about the time before I was in New York. That was a different life.

"We should probably get back to the restaurant. Our families are waiting for us. I'm sure they'll be glad to know we've agreed to their marriage plans."

Dante laughs, the sound rich and heavy. "Oh, I'm sure they're all going to be thrilled. Do you mind if we don't tell them about the part where I chased you off?"

"Deal. See, we're already doing this marriage between families thing like we're pros."

He chuckles and together we both get dressed. I quickly fix my makeup and together we head back to the restaurant to meet our families and announce that we're going to join the families.

CHAPTER 10

Iwake up the next morning at ten am, exhausted.

Dinner went well. Dante and I had spent most of it quietly eating our food while my uncle and his father discussed terms. Our mothers didn't say much, but that wasn't strange. While the women in our families were powerful, they deferred to the men in public.

After dinner, Dante and I came back to my place. There had been no taming Dante's seemingly insatiable appetite last night. Now he lays there, snoring softly on my bed. He looks adorable, which was probably his intention. I could deal with waking up to this every morning...

I start up my coffee maker and hear a sound like a Nintendo game go off in my room. *That's weird*, I think. I don't even have a TV in there. I'm halfway back to the room when I hear Dante talking.

"Yes. Yes. I know. I'll be right in," he says, talking into what had to be a cell phone. He hangs up and tosses the phone on the bed just as I step in the doorway. Blue eyes look up at me. "Business. The word is out about combining our families."

"Before you go, do you know anything about forced escorts on the north side of town?" I ask him.

He frowns and shakes his head. "My family isn't in the escorts. We dropped it a couple of years ago as it wasn't earning out. Why?"

Relief trickles through me that what happened to Sara doesn't have anything to do with Dante.

"A friend of mine had some trouble on the edge of our territories," I tell him.

His frown deepens. "I'll make sure I look into it."

"Do you want any coffee before you go?" I ask, already feeling a little domesticated by him. Next thing I know, I'll be baking cookies and pot roasts. It surprises me that I'm not dreading the idea.

He shakes his head. "No, I should get going as quickly as possible." He quickly throws his clothes on and smooths his hair. I watch him, soaking in his easy movements. He checks his pockets one last time to make sure he has everything before kissing my cheek. "See you later?"

I smile. "Count on it."

With that, he's gone, clearly in a hurry. The apartment is quiet without him. I lay back down on the bed, hoping to recover some energy before tackling the day.

I sit up with a start and quickly dial a number on my corded phone. I have to tell Ethan what happened last night before he tells Aunt Sophia.

"This is Ethan," a gruff voice I recognize answers at the second ring.

"It's Cara. I need to tell you about last night." I wait for a response, but he doesn't say anything so I just continue. "I met Dante the other day accidentally. He goes to the bar near my place. That's how he knew where to find me. He thought it was a joke that it was me there. That's why he was mad."

It's a lie, but it has enough of the truth that it will stand strong.

"That's it?" Ethan asks. "No more problems?"

"Yup. No more problems."

"Good." The line goes dead as Ethan hangs up. The man is not one for small talk.

I flop back onto the bed, ready for a nap, but less than a minute later, my phone rings. No rest for the wicked.

"Hello?" I stifle a yawn as I answer.

"Cara." The woman on the other end of the line isn't asking a question.

"May I ask who's calling?" I'm suddenly awake. I don't like unknown callers.

"It doesn't matter. There's a taxi waiting outside for you. If you know what's good for you, you'll get in it immediately."

"Who is this?" I ask, now angry. I may not be in charge yet, but I don't take orders from just anyone.

There's a sigh on the other end of the line. "My name is Victoria. I'm Dante's mother."

It's a long taxi ride out to the countryside. I think of all the things I'd rather be doing than going to meet Dante's mother, and it's a long list. Taxes, jury duty, feeding live cobras...pretty much anything, really. The taxi driver seems to be clueless, trying to make small talk with me while I'm clearly upset.

I text Aunt Sophia, but I don't get a response.

I wore my pencil skirt and a smart blouse, not really dressing up but hoping that I don't come off as a total slob. The whole way there, I think about what she could say. It clearly won't be good, her tone made that clear. Still, what's the worst that she could do to me?

When the car turns into what must be the driveway at the biggest mansion I've ever seen, I know I've arrived. The whole place screams old money. As we pull to a stop, a butler opens the door to the taxi. "Right this way, Miss Savio," he says to me. To the taxi driver, he says, "Wait here."

He leads me through corridors that seem to flaunt wealth at every opportunity. I don't recognize any of the paintings or statues, but it's obvious that they're all expensive. My current job has let me have a taste of wealth, but the displays in this house make me look like a pauper. The butler leads me to a library of some sort, full of old books. "Mrs. Russo will meet you here."

From that point on, it becomes a waiting game. I know she's looking in on me, looking for any reaction and enjoying making me uncomfortable. I sit demurely on an embroidered couch, but I can't help but be impatient. I have things to do, and the last thing I want is to be here. I keep looking at my watch, realizing that she's probably enjoying watching me get frustrated at the lost time, but I can't help myself.

After twenty minutes pass, I let out a loud sigh. The voice in my head, always the voice of reason, says *This is just a power game to her, and you don't have time for it.* I don't need this, even if she is Dante's mother. I head for the door and open it, trying to remember how to get out of here. The butler looks at me in surprise from the hallway. "Mrs. Russo will be with you shortly, please return to the room."

"I have more important things to do than wait forever," I say sharply. He doesn't react and I realize that he probably gets attitude all day from the people who live in this house. He's a working man, just like me. I smile and immediately act sweeter. "Thank you for your hospitality, sir. Please let Mrs. Russo know that the next time we meet, it will be on my terms."

I start to slip past him, but stop. There's a painting on the wall, one of a man staring out at sea. It seems to paralyze me. I see myself there, commanding the very water of the ocean. I could be that powerful.

I'm about to leave when I hear footsteps behind me. "I thought you had important things to do," a woman's voice says.

I shrug without looking back. "I have time to admire art."

She stands next to me. I can smell her perfume before I see her, and it makes her smell old and rich. Her red dress is flattering, but again screams more money than taste. "Then you have time to talk to me, too."

"What do you want? Or did you just want me to see your expensive artwork?" I motion to the painting. The waves seem to move as the man commands them. Whatever she paid for that painting was worth it.

She grimaces and I get the feeling that this isn't a topic that she wants to talk about. "No. I asked you here to tell you that you cannot marry Dante."

I nearly laugh. "That's up to the families. I thought you wanted this marriage."

"My husband wants this marriage," she corrects me. "I know Dante. I want him to be happy. And that isn't with you. You marry him, and I'll make sure your life is miserable."

I stare at her in disbelief. I don't really have many options here. I can marry Dante, be happy, but she'll make my life miserable or I can leave Dante, be sad, and my family will make my life miserable.

It's a pretty easy choice for me to make.

"You really should discuss this with my aunt and uncle," I tell her. "You should probably talk to your husband about this as well."

She grimaces as I call her bluff.

"I have. I'm trying to do what's best for my son," she tells me. "He deserves someone better."

I'm sure there's a certain someone that she wants instead. There's always power plays between families. She probably made a deal with another family and is now feeling the squeeze.

"I'll make sure you're invited to the wedding," I say, feeling powerful. I turn in what I hope is the direction out.

I can also destroy your life. Do you understand me?" I can feel her glittering with malice behind me. "I will *destroy* you."

I sigh loudly and dramatically. "Are we done here?"

She walks in front of me, her heels clicking on the floor as she faces me, giving me the first really good look of her face. She looks like someone who was once very pretty, and very high society. However, now she looks tired, like the weight of the world is on her shoulders. "Of course. You can expect another call from me very soon. I will find something on you."

I smile back. "I hope it'll be to congratulate Dante and I on our pending nuptials." I turn and walk toward the door before I can see her reaction, but I am sure it isn't happy.

Desperate people do desperate things. I wonder why she doesn't want what everyone else does.

CHAPTER 11

I have the taxi driver drop me off a few blocks from my house, knowing that I need the time to think things over. The cold, crisp air outside feels good against my hot cheeks. It smells like it might snow later and I secretly hope for a blizzard. A physical cage of snow sounds better than the threatened cage Victoria Russo has just put me in.

At least if there was a blizzard, I could spend the time going through my apartment searching and removing the recording devices that were probably hidden in my apartment. That was the only way she could have known that Dante had left or was even there in the first place. She would certainly have the motive and the funds to do so.

I kick an empty can down the sidewalk, listening to it plink and ping against the frozen concrete. There's the steady hum of traffic beside me and the cold wind of winter whistling through the buildings. I take a deep breath, focusing on how the cold feels in my lungs. I'm only wearing the skirt and blouse, but I'm hot with anger. I take another breath, filling myself with the icy wind. It makes my insides ache and gives me something physical to concentrate on.

My mind is still having trouble wrapping around my encounter with Mrs. Russo. I didn't see it coming and that scares me. I'm usually good at seeing things like this. I've been trained by my family to look for things. It's part of running a business.

I wonder if I'm losing my skills.

I turn the corner past my building, still full of anxious, angry energy. I have to come up with a plan. I hate being surprised and Victoria Russo has certainly surprised me. Someone must have dirt on her. She had to have a good reason for going against her husband on this.

I walk faster, pumping blood through my legs and watching my breath mist the air. I don't even have an actual destination, just a need for movement. With my body occupied, my mind is free to tumble and turn and work on the problem on hand.

What do I feel for Dante? Am I just doing this out of family obligation, or do I truly care about him? I'm not sure. I know I'm not cut out for a future of happiness and love. I'm pretty sure that he isn't either. Does that make us the perfect pair, then? We would never be content in a white-picket fenced yard with two kids and a dog, but I can see us as the two most powerful people in New York. We could make this work.

I step out onto the crosswalk only to have a cab scream past, horn blaring as it misses me by a mere inch. I stumble back onto the sidewalk, heart in my throat. The big red hand glares at me from across the street, admonishing me for even thinking of walking. I was so caught up in my thoughts that I hadn't been paying attention. I run my fingers through my hair, trying to center myself.

If I'm going to survive this I need to pay attention.

"You okay?" a small voice asks from beside me. "You look like you don't feel good."

I look down and see a girl looking up at me with big brown eyes. She's probably around twelve-years-old, but she has on light makeup, making her look slightly older. She's no longer a child. She looks so innocent, yet ready for adulthood. It's like looking back through time at a picture of myself. I suddenly notice the cold air.

"I... uh..." I stammer, trying to find the words, but her eyes – the same shape and shade as my own – have me completely unable to form a sentence.

A woman with long brown hair and kind blue eyes puts her hands on the little girl's shoulders. "I'm so sorry if she's bothering you," the woman apologizes. She squeezes the girl's shoulders as only a mother can. She's wearing a yellow sweater. "She's just very friendly."

"No, she's fine," I manage to mumble. The girl smiles and I'm suddenly transported back in time. Memories hit me hard and fast. My lungs refuse to work. Panic, fear, heartache, and loss all fight in my stomach like rabid monsters. I feel like I'm going to be sick. "I have to go..."

I step out into the street just as the light changes. A cab leans on its horn as I barely miss a collision with the yellow and black door, but I don't care. I have to get away from her. I can't be near her.

I stumble for three blocks, turning at every opportunity to get away from the girl. She's me in another timeline and I feel fear like a physical hand on my skin.

Looking at her is like looking at a broken dream. Even with her safely three blocks behind me, I can feel her eyes asking me, "*Why?*"

I don't like my answer.

A lone tear trickles down my cheek. It's hot at first, but cools quickly by the winter wind. I wipe it away, and then stare at the damp spot on the palm of my hand. I thought I had shed all my tears over my past. I thought I had left it all behind me. I glance back at the road, expecting to see the girl like a ghost haunting me, but the street is full of adult strangers. The past still haunts me, no matter how fast I run or how well I hide.

I need a drink. Or a good fuck. Something to take my mind off the little girl I once was. I know where I can get both.

My hands shake as I take a quarter out of my pocket and step into the first phone booth I see. My fingers are numb with the cold but the plastic box seems hot in comparison to the temperature outside. I dial Dante's number and hold the receiver up to my ear.

"Go," comes the gruff response on the other line.

"Dante?" My voice comes out squeakier than I had intended. I'm far more rattled than I care to admit.

"Vesper?" His tone softens with concern. "Are you all right?"

"I need to see you." I have control of myself again, even if my hand is shaking. I tell myself it's just from the cold.

"Okay," Dante says. "I just need to finish up some paper-work and then I can meet you-"

"No," I cut him off. "I can't wait. I need you now."

"You need me now, eh?" There is a smile and pride in his voice. "You can come to my office then."

He gives me his address. I don't have anything to write it down on, so I just memorize it instead. It's only a few blocks away, so I'm not worried about forgetting it. I've been there before for business. I think of Dante's bare chest instead of the little girl. That's what I want. I hang up the phone and start walking, letting the fires of need keep me warm against the winter wind.

CHAPTER 12

The lobby of Dante's office is almost eerily quiet, which given that it was the middle of the day isn't that strange, but the silence is still unnerving. A lone security guard looks up from the desk as I open the door and approach. There isn't another way to get to the shiny silver elevators, so I go straight up him.

The desk is situated in such a way that it makes it feel as though the guard is looming over me. The big man stares down his long nose as if I were a bug on the floor, but I don't care. I have done this enough times to know how to behave.

"I'm Vesper. I'm here to see Mr. Dante Russo. He's expecting me." I stand with my hand on my hip, confident and tall. Nobody intimidates me.

The guard blinks slowly and then nods toward the elevator without saying a word. The silence actually makes him more daunting than if he had spoken, but he isn't my problem anymore. I walk to the elevator, feeling his eyes on my ass the whole way. I make sure to sashay just a little bit.

It's a long ride up to Dante's office on the 47th floor. My ears pop with the height increase and I swear I can feel the building sway in the wind as I step out of the elevator. The hallway is painted in a neutral tan that all businesses seem to prefer. His family must be doing well to afford all this. I know that the Russos are big in real estate.

I find the heavy wooden door with his suite number. The placard is blank on the door, as if he doesn't want anyone to know he is here. I can't say I blame him. Given his status, he probably has people bothering him all the time. The office building is nice, but definitely not the trendiest. This would be a good place to work without having wannabe clients harassing him all day.

The door opens on smooth hinges and I step inside. The lobby is bare with only a couple of tired, gray waiting room chairs. I walk through it to the only door that looks like it might contain something. I knock this time and the sound seems to echo through the room.

"Come in," Dante says through the door. I push it open, unsure of what I'm going to find.

This room looks entirely different than the threadbare lobby. A lamp in the corner gives off a warm light that makes the room comfortable and welcoming, especially after the dismal, gray entrance. Dante stands at the window, peeking through the closed blinds at the street below. He's wearing a suit and jacket, and it's kind of weird. It's like he's wearing his father's clothes.

A heavy, black desk fills the center of the room with a comfortable-looking leather chair behind it. Two book-shelves filled to the brim line the walls along with a filing cabinet and two paintings of seascapes.

I'm hot. After walking in the cold in that skirt, the heated room is making my cold hands prickle.

I head straight for Dante. I need him to fill me, to take my mind away from the girl and from Victoria.

"Hey, what's the matter?" he asks.

"Shut up and kiss me," I say, coming around the desk.

As we kiss, I can see his own hunger begin to rise within him. I unbutton and shrug out of my blouse, letting it fall to the ground. There's a burning in my core in a way that only he can put out. I can feel how excited he's getting already. His hands go behind me for my bra, unclasping it and letting it drop to the floor. I can't wait, I practically attack him. I have to get the image of that little girl out of my mind.

"I want you to fuck me, Dante. Not make love to me," I whisper in his ear. I need this. I need him to take me away from myself. I don't want a gentle love-making session. I want something that mixes pleasure and pain and makes me forget about everything. I need it hard and I need it now.

He pulls away from me a little bit. "Are you sure?" I can see the dark hunger swirling in his eyes.

I bite my lip and smile, nodding. "Take me, Dante. I'm yours to take as you want."

His eyes darken and he suddenly seems taller. He grabs my hair and pulls me to his desk. I sit on the edge of the wood, arching my back and thrusting out my chest. I want to tempt him. I moan loudly, just wanting nothing but his cock inside of me. He leaves one hand in my hair while the other one begins to hike up my skirt.

He caresses my inner thigh, working his fingers up the sensitive flesh to the cloth of my panties. Without warning, he slips a finger into me. Luckily, I want him bad enough that I have a little lubrication, but not nearly enough to make the penetration pleasurable. I wince. "Careful..." I whine as I look back at him.

He removes his hand and sticks the finger in his mouth, savoring my flavor. His face is emotionless while his eyes burn with a lust I don't recognize. "You said to take you. You sure you want to continue?"

I swallow hard. His erection is huge against my leg. "Yes," I whisper, looking at his pants.

He scrunches his hand in my hair, forcing me to stand and turn so he can push me down onto the desk. He's stronger than me but I don't fight back when he pushes down on my low back and rips my skirt down my legs. My nipples harden against the cold of his desk.

"Stay there," he commands. This isn't the Dante I know. It's his voice, but it doesn't sound like the Bond I met in the piano bar. Still, I'm so turned on I just hug his desk.

I feel his hands behind me, suddenly wrapping his fingers around the crotch of my panties and tearing. A mixture of fear and arousal spikes my heart rate he pulls the pieces of my panties down each leg, keeping just a strip of the fabric holding it together. He traces a finger down my spine, down the line of my butt and to the v between my legs. I spread my legs wide to give him access. He forces one finger inside of me, but this time I'm ready. I'm already so wet. I want more than just a finger. I start to moan. "Dante..."

"Shut up," he growls. His finger drops away, leaving me aching for more. I hear his footsteps go to the front of the desk and I raise my head to look at him, but he grabs a handful of my hair and pulls up. I squeak with surprise and pain as he forces my head up. His crotch is right at eye level for me and his pants are unbuttoned and open. When I look up at his face, he just smiles. "Make sure to get it nice and wet."

I do what he says, taking it in my mouth. He begins to fuck my mouth roughly, lubricating it, taking what he wants. My breasts stick to the surface of the desk as I raise and lower my head. My core is made of fire and this is stoking the heat. Tears spring from my eyes when he goes too deep, but I'm loving every minute of it. This is what I wanted. What I needed.

He steps back and goes back around to the other side of the desk. I get on my tiptoes, opening myself up for him. His hard length leans against my ass, and he poises himself at my damp entrance. He pushes into me, making it feel good for him. It immediately scratches the itch, and I find myself rocking back at him.

He puts his hand on my back, holding me down. He's fucking me hard, ramming his entire length as deep into me as he can go. It's violent and rough, but I love it. It's making me forget my past.

His hand traces the curve of my low back continuing to palm my ass. He spreads my cheeks wide, watching as he plows into me. He pulls out of me and grabs my hair again. I stumble to my feet as he drags me toward the window, my torn panties trying to trip me as I walk. At one point I stumble, but he just keeps going, pulling my hair with him and causing me pain as well as pleasure. I love it. I want more.

He pushes me onto his desk, pinning my arms above my head as he rails into me. My head hangs off the edge, pleasure finally taking over the memories that threaten to crush me. This is real. This is now. I don't have to worry about what happened then.

"More," I whisper. I'm so close to losing myself to him. It's a drug to forget and he's getting me high on him.

Dante thrusts harder, his body slamming into mine. There's raw power and hungry lust fueling him now. He's now primal and needy. I welcome it.

I feel him start to shake, his body finding the ultimate pleasure in mine. This is what I need. This is where I need to be right now.

I close my eyes and take all of him. The guttural sound of him coming sends me over the edge, and my body contracts around him.

We stay that way for a long time, locked together and

breathing hard. Slowly he steps back. I lay panting on his desk.

"Are you okay?" Dante asks, his eyes still on me.

I slide to the floor. Now that we're done, the memories are coming back. They aren't as overpowering this time.

"I think so," I whisper. He wraps his arms around me. Somehow, the gentle strength of his arms after the intense strength of before is more soothing than anything I could have expected. I let him hold me, and slowly the memories of an unwanted kiss that led to my mother's death start to fade.

"I want to go home," I whisper, suddenly empty of energy. I just want to curl up in my bed.

"I'll take you home myself," he says, gently smoothing back my hair.

I nod. He helps me dress and then brings me downstairs. He calls a cab and lets me rest on his shoulder the whole way home without saying a word.

He tucks me into bed with a kiss.

I know that I am safe with him.

CHAPTER 13

"Where exactly are we going?" I ask two days later, peering out from the limousine window. My breath is fogging the icy glass and making it hard to see.

"I told you, it's a surprise," Dante answers nonchalantly, leaning back in his leather seat. His white button-up shirt is open at the collar and I am strongly considering opening it further. The backseat of a limo has plenty of room and privacy for where I want this date to go. He shakes his head slowly, his brown eyes knowing exactly what I am planning. I have to wait.

I slump back in my own seat and cross my arms. I know I look like a irritable, spoiled brat. Dante rolls his eyes, but a sliver of a grin cracks his face. I can tell at least he is considering my idea.

"We're here," he says as the car pulls to a stop. "Behave and later we can play."

The way he says the word play sends a small shiver down my spine. I like it when we play.

The door to the limo opens and the driver helps me out. I

leave my coat in the car and my breath catches in the cold afternoon air. Dante is right behind me and I can feel his warmth. In front of us is the Hayden Sphere. I'd seen it, but have never been inside. I know it is part of the American Museum of Natural History and that they just redid it a year or so ago. It looks like a clear cube with a giant ball inside. It certainly makes me think of something from space.

"The planetarium?" I ask, turning my head to look at Dante. He grins.

"You said you never get to see the stars anymore," he explained, wrapping his arm around my shoulder and guiding me toward the building. "Well, this afternoon we are going to see some stars."

I barely remember saying that in passing. I'm impressed he remembered at all. The clear night sky is something I miss from my old life. I am more than happy to trade those small twinkling lights in the sky for the sparkling lights of the city.

We enter the the glass doors of the museum and start to wander through the exhibits. I'm not really paying attention to Jupiter's red spot or even that Pluto isn't given its rightful place as a planet anymore. I'm focused on Dante.

His hand is on my shoulder as we read an exhibit display. It's hot through my thin, silk blouse. I close my eyes and try to think, but all I can concentrate on is how good it feels to have him touch me. For a moment, I let myself dream. The two of us, married and happy. A wedding with me in a white dress and him waiting at the end of the aisle.

Except, as I walk down the aisle in my thoughts, Victoria Russo is there. Her cold eyes pierce my happy thoughts and ruin my imaginary wedding. I open my eyes and let Dante guide me to the next display. I need to talk to Aunt Sophia about her.

The museum is blissfully quiet with only a couple of other patrons browsing the exhibits. It seems strange to see anywhere in New York quiet, but it is a weekday. A small boy, no older than four years old, points up at one of the planets lining the museum and shouts with glee. His mother smiles and picks him up, keeping his excitement in check. He is the only child here. It must just be a slower day until school lets out and the children come flocking to see the planets.

"Are you close with your parents?" I ask Dante, watching the mother whisper to her child about the stars. The happy duo look like something from a sappy Mother's Day card commercial.

"I'm a good son," Dante answers noncommittally, his eyes following mine to the mother and child. It's slight, but his jaw tightens. "I know where my family loyalties lie."

"Do you talk to your mom a lot?" I keep my voice light and easy, even though my heart is squeezing into my throat. I want him to say no. I want him to say that he doesn't listen to a thing she says and that the woman has no real power over him. I want the conversation with her to be nothing but an empty threat.

Dante turns his full attention to me. There's something ancient and dark in those dark eyes. His face is hard and I know I'm treading on dangerous ground with this subject. "She runs the Russo Family and she is my mother."

I try to smile like it was just an innocent question, but my heart sinks a little. *She runs the Russo Family...* which means she has power over him. For a moment, I wonder if we're going about this all too fast. There are too many ways that Victoria can sabotage this.

Dante walks to the next display, leaving me to catch up. The edge is gone from his voice and the easy-going smile of youth crosses his features as I join him. "What about you? You close with your parents?"

"They're dead, so not really," I say, bitterness making my

words short. "Sophia is my mother's sister. She took me in when my mother died."

"I'm sorry," Dante says, wrapping his arm around me. He's warm and I am safe. For a moment, I wish that we were different people. I wish that we were normal. That we didn't have the family pushing us together or anyone wanting us to stay apart. I wished that this could be a boring story without any of the danger or stress.

"It was a long time ago," I say.

He kisses my head and smooths my hair with his hand. "Any siblings?"

"No. My dad died when I was a toddler and my mother never remarried."

"A brother and a sister," he answers, but doesn't offer up any more information.

He guides us to the next display. I wasn't finished reading the last one, but I go with him anyway. It takes me three steps to realize that he's been subtly moving us through the museum on a schedule. I didn't even realize he had been doing it. Something about the ease of which he moves me along bothers me. I don't like not being in control. If we're to be married and our families joined, I need to be in control as much as he is.

"You said you used to be able to see the stars," Dante says, pointing to a display with a picture of North America. "Where did you live?"

I know he doesn't mean anything by the question. It's something that a fiance should know about their betrothed, but it irks me. I should be glad that he hasn't pried into my life and found out all of this from other people. He's asking me, yet I don't want to talk about it.

Unjustified anger heats my center. The fact that it's unjustified just makes it worse and now I'm angry at myself too.

"It doesn't matter. There's no one there to go home to." The only person left in that town is the one person in this world I need to run from. They are the person that killed my mother.

I want to snap at him, but that isn't fair. I take a deep breath. It isn't his fault that I have a tragic past. I remind myself that he's in love with me and that I am in love with him.

"Dante..." I turn to look at him, and my heart aches. His dark brow is tight and it just makes him more beautiful. "It's not that interesting. Or important."

"It is to me," he says, taking my hands.

I sigh. I don't like talking about this. I don't like thinking about that day.

"I grew up in the suburbs outside of Detroit," I say softly. "It was just my mother and me. She didn't want to be in the mattress business. She was a professional piano player. She was amazing. People would come from all over to hear her play."

Dante's hands are warm around mine. I concentrate on that.

"She started seeing this guy. He seemed like a good choice. He was campaigning to be senator. I thought he loved my mother, but..." My voice falters a little. In the eyes of an adult, the issues are easy to see, but the eyes of a child are blind. "He wasn't a good person. My mother would come home with bruises. She told me it was always an accident."

Dante's hands tighten and I can see anger flash in his eyes.

"Anyway, it was a week after my twelfth birthday. He drove me home from school. My mother wasn't home." My shoulders tighten with the memory. It's taken years to work through this moment. Sometimes, I wake screaming from nightmares where I relive this moment. "He kissed me. He touched my chest and said I was growing up into a such a lovely young woman. I tried to leave the car, but he grabbed me. He left bruises on my arm. He hurt me when I didn't give him what he wanted."

Dante growls. He's angry for me.

"I told my mother. She was furious. It was her breaking point. She was leaving him. She had me pack a bag while she went to tell him it was the end. She said she'd destroy him for this. She died in a car crash on the way home."

I leave out the lingering questions I have about her death. I've tried to figure out how it happened, but it never seems to make sense. I've read the reports. I've even been to the site of the accident. It doesn't feel right. The words in the report don't match what I saw. Something about it makes me uncomfortable. I have no actual proof that he killed her, but I can't seem to shake the feeling either. I just know that some-how, John Norwood is responsible for her death.

"I'm so sorry," he says, his hands still tight on mine.

"Uncle Tony and Aunt Sophia took me in. They made me their own." I'm more confident with this part. This part doesn't make my chest feel too tight. This part is where I feel safe again. "Family means everything to me now. They saved me from him. He's a powerful man and he wasn't pleased when they took me. They made sure I was safe and well cared for."

"Oh, Vesper," Dante whispers my name. Concern replaces the anger in his eyes. He touches my face and I realize I'm crying. The pads of his fingers smear the tear across my cheek.

"I don't want to tell you because it isn't who I am anymore. I don't want you to look at me differently." I wish my voice didn't waver so much, but I can't help it. I don't like being this emotionally exposed to anyone. He wants to marry me and the small voice in the back of my mind keeps telling me that if he finds out who I really am, he will leave and never come back. I know that it's not true, but that doesn't stop the insecurities from whispering through my mind. "Can you understand?"

"Yes," he says, pulling me into his chest and wrapping his arms around me. I relax into him, feeling safe for a moment.

"You have any dark past I need to know about?" I ask him.

"I'm in the mob," he whispers, making me giggle.

I feel a little better now.

"Would you still like to see the stars?" Dante asks after a moment. "I mean, I get it if you don't... the stars being part of your past and all."

I ignore the implication of his words. "No, I'd like to see them. Stars don't have pasts."

"What?" One of Dante's dark brows lifts. We start walking toward the planetarium entrance.

"I guess it doesn't matter with projected stars," I say, motioning to the rounded ceiling as we enter. "But, for real stars, the light we see in the sky is millions of years old. The light left its star around the time of the dinosaurs and has traveled through space for all that time and we're just seeing it now. We're seeing something that doesn't exist anymore. The past and the future doesn't matter to stars because it's all the same. Time is meaningless to them."

Dante nods as if he understands, but I don't think he does. Some days, it barely makes sense to me, but I find comfort in the stars and how they don't experience time. My life doesn't matter to a star and something about that is soothing.

He gently guides me past the rings of chairs angled up to see the domed roof and to the center of the room. We're obviously not supposed to sit here, but he pulls me down to the ground. I reluctantly sit, watching as he lays down on the floor and puts his hands behind his head. The motion makes the muscles of his arms stand out in a way that makes my mouth go dry with want.

"Aren't we supposed to be in the chairs?" I look around, but no one else is coming in the room.

"Nope." He grins, looking charming and boyish. His hair is just about to fall into his eyes, so I gently brush it off his forehead. He closes his eyes at my touch, practically purring like a cat. "This is all ours for the hour. You can sit wherever you want." He opens one eye and glances at the space next to him, indicating where he thinks I should sit.

I nestle in closer to him, drawing his strength into me. The lights dim and the sky suddenly fills with stars. It's so real for a moment I forget where I am. I can feel Dante's heartbeat, strong and steady under me. I close my eyes and let myself relax into him for a moment. I let myself truly fall in love with Dante.

I know I won't stop loving him after this moment. Once you love Dante Russo, you will never stop loving him.

CHAPTER 14

The heat when I open the door makes me sigh in relief after hurrying through the cold morning fog. Sara is waiting for me in our usual booth at the diner. The whole place smells like pancakes and coffee and it's making my mouth water.

"You're late," Sara chastises me as I sit down across from her and wrap my chilled hands around the cup of coffee she has waiting for me. The heat burns through my frozen fingers but I don't let go.

"Sorry," I mumble. "I had a hard time getting up this morning."

"Late night?" she asks, sipping on her own coffee. She's gorgeous again today. Her blonde hair is pulled back into a ponytail that curls down her back. Her dark maroon shirt is long sleeved but low cut enough to display a generous amount of cleavage, but not to the point of being slutty. The haggard, frightened girl I met last time in this diner is gone.

"Actually, I went to bed early last night. I just didn't sleep very good." I pick up a sugar packet and play with it. "Too much on my mind."

"Your upcoming wedding partner?" she teases.

"Him and half a dozen other people," I reply. I can't believe how tired I am and take a big sip of coffee.

"You're keeping everything bottled up inside again, Miss Cara Savio." Sara takes a sip of her coffee and leans back in her chair. "Talk to me. Let it out."

"It's all family business," I tell her. "Uncle Tony is having me take on more responsibilities. I'm doing a lot of the work integrating the two families. We're not just merging people, we're merging businesses. It's a lot of work."

"I bet," she says, sipping at her coffee. "There's still more. I can tell."

"I found out it wasn't the Russos with your escort trouble," I say with a shrug. "I'm still digging as to who thought it was a good idea to try taking a girl on my turf, though."

She shudders a little.

"I won't let that happen again," I promise. "I made sure to put some guys up there to keep things under control. Ethan says he'll help."

"Thanks," she says, and sips her coffee. "I'm okay now. I'm strong." She looks up at me. "And you aren't getting me off topic that easily. There's something else bothering you. Something big."

I play with my coffee cup, twisting it around in my hands. I glance around, but no one is nearby. I have to tell someone or I'll go crazy.

"The Russo family is split on the marriage," I finally whisper. "You can't tell anyone."

"What? Seriously?" Her eyes go wide. "I mean, I won't tell a soul. I thought they wanted the families to merge."

"His mother is against the marriage," I reply. "She wants me to break it off."

"And have both the Savios and the Russos hate you? Yeah,

that sounds like a good plan," she says sarcastically. "Why doesn't she want you to marry him?"

"I have no idea. She says it's not a good match or something." I shrug.

"How did you find this out?"

"She had a taxi pick me up and take me to her house. It's a freaking mansion. I didn't know how loaded the Russos were." I sip at my coffee.

"You know it's all for show, right?" Sara asks.

"What do you mean?"

"They're old school mafia. They have roots in Sicily or something, but they made most of their money in real estate in the early eighties. They had a trash company and were basically the stereotypical Italian mafia," Sara explains. "That's why they have that big house, the buildings, stuff like that. But, they're not making money like they used to. The money is in digital now, which is why they want in on the Savio Family."

"Where did you learn all that?" I ask. I'm impressed that she's delved into the histories of the families.

"It's interesting. There's a couple other organizations that the Russos could have chosen. The Romanos in New Jersey, the Moretti Family, and the Scutari Family. But, none of them are as successful as the Savios."

I raise my eyebrows in surprise. "You still haven't told me how you learned all this," I tell her.

She blushes. "I'm kind of seeing somebody."

"Yeah?" I'm happy for her. "What's the lucky guy's name?"

She chews on her lip for a second. "You have to promise to stay quiet about it. It's new and I don't know if it's long term and I don't want to cause problems."

"Who is it?" I grin. I'm thinking maybe one of the Maroni brothers. They were at all the family functions, and I actually thought the older one was pretty cute. "What's his name?"

"Ethan."

She says his name and it doesn't register in my head. Ethan is probably five or ten years older than Sara. I don't actually know his age, just that he was military and is a scary enforcer.

"Ethan? Like, the guy who keeps me safe Ethan?"

Her shoulders fall a little. "Yeah. I can tell you're not happy about it."

I shake my head. "No, it's not that. I just..." I shrug. "I just am surprised you got him to say more than three words in a sentence."

She relaxes a little. "He's actually pretty smart."

"Well, if he's dating you, then I can see that," I say with a nod. Ethan and I don't usually talk much.

"You won't say anything, will you?" Sara fiddles with her coffee cup. "It's still really new."

"You like him, though, right?"

A smile crosses her face and her eyes light up a little. "Yeah."

It's obvious that she's thinks he the best thing since sliced bread. It's not a match I would have made, but if it makes her happy, then I'm glad.

"You know what he does for a living, right?" I ask her.

"Yeah." She shrugs. "But, he's on my side. He's a good man."

Yeah. Just dangerous as fuck.

"I'm happy for you two," I tell her. "But, please don't tell me sex stories with him. I don't think I could look at him the same."

Sara laughs and the tension is gone. We're friends again.

"Maybe Dante's mom had a deal with another family," she says suddenly. "Like, she promised Dante to the Romanos, but the rest of the family went with the Savios."

It sounds plausible. "Maybe. I don't know. It's just weird." I finish my cup of coffee. "We should order. I'm starving."

"Sounds good."

Sara smiles at me and we start talking about normal every day things again. Still, her idea about Dante's mother stays with me. It's probably just that I want things to make sense, but there's something about it that keeps tugging on my mind the rest of breakfast.

After breakfast, I wander around the city for a little while, looking at shops and doing my best not to think. The Christmas decorations are out on display and it's easy to lose myself to the green and red of the season. I don't buy anything. I'm a ghost just floating through the city, trying to figure out what to do next.

I head home once I'm cold and tired. My bed welcomes me with open arms and the promise of release from my thoughts. When I lay my head down on the pillow, I smell Dante. He had just been here two days ago, and his scent still lingers all over the place. I smile as I snuggle into the pillow, imagining his hard body is what I'm holding onto.

My dreams are terrible, as they often are. Dreams of my mother, dreams of the car accident, dreams of the worst futures I can imagine for myself.

I wake up at what seems like dawn to my phone ringing. I answer it with sleep still in my voice. "Hello?"

"Cara." It was Mrs. Russo's horrible voice.

"Can I help you?" I ask, ready to just turn off my phone so she couldn't call me back.

"Oh, I just thought we could admire some art again today."

I pause. Is this some kind of game to her? "No, thanks, I'm kind of busy today."

"Oh, please, Cara. I'll have you home in plenty of time for your little meeting tonight." There is laughter in her voice, as if she's mocking me. "I just really wanted to talk to you about this piece I found. It's something Senator Norwood is letting me borrow. I think your mother would have been interested in it..." She trails off.

"Leave me alone, okay?" I yell into the phone without thinking.

I hear her *tsk tsk*. "That's no way to talk to your potential mother-in-law. I just thought you might want to talk about this little girl before I showed it to Dante."

Fury courses through my mind. "Fine!" I say through gritted teeth.

"Fantastic!" she says, way too happy. "There's a taxi waiting outside."

My stomach does flip flops for the entire taxi ride. I wonder what she could possibly have. Senator Norwood. Just hearing his name is like being dipped in dark water. He killed my mother and now Victoria Russo is using it to make me do what she wants. This can't be happening.

When the taxi arrives at the mansion, the butler opens my door, just as he did last time. A loyal servant is something that every rich person needs, I think to myself.

This time, when the butler steers me into the library, I don't put up a fight. I know that she's got the power now, and I know that she's going to remind me of it every chance she gets.

I sit and fidget in the chair. My hands are shaking and I think I might throw up. I try to think of what I'll say, but I don't know what link she found to my old life. Still, if she is watching me, she already knows how nervous I am. I do my best to hide it even more.

A full thirty minutes later, the butler comes in with a cup of tea. Whether ordered to or just out of the goodness of his heart, he smiles as he hands it to me. I'm sure he has seen his fair share of people that Victoria Russo has screwed with before. I don't object to the wait this time, I simply thank him for the tea.

Five minutes after that, Mrs. Russo finally walks in. "Ah, thank you for waiting, my dear." She looks like the cat that found the cream as she takes the seat across from mine.

I wait for her to talk, but she just relaxes into the chair more. I feel like she's waiting for me to talk, but I don't want to prompt her too much about my past life, so I say nothing. The silence is stifling and I can't stand it. I break.

"This is nice," I say facetiously.

"Hmm," a thin smile crosses her face.

I decide to twist the knife a little. "I might inherit this mansion someday."

"Oh, I doubt that very much, dear," she says sweetly, but I get the feeling that she'd rather burn the place to the ground than let me live in it. There's another pause, then she leans forward. "Come now, dear. I sense a little bit of a kindred spirit, and it would be a shame if we couldn't talk like civilized ladies."

A nervous little laugh escapes me, but I compose myself. "Okay, let's talk."

She waits for me to say more, but I don't have anything more forthcoming. "I'll start then. I can't have you bringing your drama into my family. Lord knows that we have enough already."

I believe her when she says there's a lot of drama, and I figure that she probably causes the bulk of it. "Dante loves me, so I'm afraid you'll just have to deal with it. It's done."

She sits back again, that infuriating smile never leaving her face. "I have a deal to make with you."

I narrow my eyes. I have no intention of doing anything this woman wants, but I'm willing to listen. It might prove useful. "I'm listening," I tell her.

"You see, people work best when given a carrot and a stick. Something positive to motivate them, as well as a threat. I'm sure you've heard this before," she says, crossing her legs.

"So which are you offering me? The carrot or the stick?" I cross my arms.

"Both, dear. Both." She smiles again, but it's cold. She stands up and crosses the room, walking slowly and enjoying the attention. "You tell my son it's off. That you've changed your mind. The families will get over it. I'll make sure there is no repercussion on our end."

Yeah right, I say to myself. *There will be plenty of repercussion.*

"So what's the carrot and the stick?"

"I had the most interesting conversation the other day with the woman that was John Norwood's secretary around the time he was seeing your mother." She says it nonchalantly, but the words make my chest tighten.

What if the secretary knew something about my mother's death? I still believe it wasn't an accident. Curiosity starts to crowd into my thoughts.

"She said some very interesting things," Victoria continues. She makes eye contact with me. "Very interesting. Especially about the accident."

"So the carrot is information on my mother's accident."

"On your mother's supposed accident."

My heart leaps into my throat.

"And the stick?" I ask.

"I tell Senator Norwood where the proof is so he can destroy it." Her smile is cruel. "You see? A carrot and a stick."

She's right. I want the information, but not at this price. I don't even know if this is valid information. It's not exactly a secret that my family thinks my mother was murdered. The senator is a powerful man. He was more powerful than my uncle at the time. Given that the senator wants to run for president, he's only gotten more powerful since I last saw him.

"I'll think about it," I manage to say.

"Don't think too long. I haven't told the senator I know anything yet, but, well..." she pauses, then smiles at me again. "I'll need an answer pretty soon."

I act like her threat frightens me, when all it does is convince me that she wants me to make a hasty decision before thinking it out. Victoria would make a formidable poker player, but I'd take the prize home every night from her. I nod, then stand to leave.

"Oh, and, Cara?" I turn back to look at her. She's practically cawing with pride over winning. "I know my son doesn't care for me much, and I'm alright with that. However, don't think that the two of you can beat me together. You can't. If you try, I'll destroy you both."

I nod, still managing to look frightened. On the inside, I'm smiling. She's afraid that Dante can beat her, and that's why she doesn't want me to bring this to Dante. Plans are already starting to form in my head, and I can't get out of there fast enough.

I see the butler on the way out. He makes eye contact with me, looking grave. I can't help but crack a small smile, hoping that he'll see that I haven't been broken yet.

CHAPTER 16

The piano beckons me with black and white fingers. I sit and raise the lid without having to think about what I'm doing. I start with a simple scale and arpeggio, letting the easy motions flow. My fingers climb the keys, finding harmony and balance while my mind scrambles.

My mother's killer. My mother's death resolved.

Another scale cascades from my fingertips. The beauty is harsh against my reality.

I see Dante's blue eyes when I close mine. How do I tell him what his mother is doing? Family is everything to people like us. I don't want to cause problems.

What if Senator Norwood did kill my mother? What would I do then?

My hands falter despite the ease of the scale and I have to restart the scale. It's been ten years but he still frightens me. I still have nightmares of him coming to the city and finding me. He has only grown more powerful with time and made more political friends. He ruined my life once and still has the power to do it again. I know I'm not the scared twelve-year-old girl anymore, but I'm not sure if I'll remember that when faced with him.

Or what he could do to Dante. Dante's business was much less legally gray than mine. He could destroy him and the entire Russo family. He would destroy Dante if he thought it would help him. Since Dante is connected to me, I know that he would think it amusing to tear the Russo family down using me. Victoria might just meet her match if she tries to involve him.

I stop playing as I can't remember what scale comes next. I don't know what comes next for me either. It feels strange to have a such a powerful sense of urgency and yet know I have time. I have time to respond to Victoria, time before she gives me the evidence or destroys it, time to decide what I want-- but I know it will never be enough time. This is a decision I never want to make and I will never have enough time to decide. All I have is time and yet I don't have enough of it.

I start a classical piece that I know by heart. The familiar melodies are soothing and I can almost let my mind settle enough to think clearly.

What if I take Victoria's offer? What if I get the evidence to prove my mother was murdered? Would it soothe this ache on my soul? I don't know, but I do know that I want justice. My mother deserves that much.

Except Dante.

My fingers slip and I sour the passage. I know this piece well enough to do it in my sleep, but just thinking of leaving Dante makes me forget what I've always known. He changes everything. Those dark eyes and the warmth of his smile make me want only him.

Thoughts of the man I'm falling in love with and my mother war in my head. Two people that I love. I have to choose.

My hands hover over the piano. I've gone through all my scales and the warm-up pieces. I have to make a choice: do I attempt a new song or go with something I know and am good at?

Instead. I close the piano lid.

If you don't like the game, change the rules.

So that's what I'm going to do.

CHAPTER 17

"I'm so glad I was able to attend your fundraiser, Mr. Senator Grayson," I say, making my voice low and sexy. To be honest, this had been one of my better business meetings. I had actually enjoyed the conversation part of the evening. I just wished Dante had been here with me.

I'm at a dinner fundraiser for Senator Grayson. The Savio Family bought out two tables. Only I came, but I made political connections. The heir to the mattress empire is someone everyone wants on their side.

Senator Grayson's not bad looking for a man over sixty, but it's his influence and power that makes him attractive. As the head of his political party, he can change policy with the raise of an eyebrow. He's exactly the kind of person that I want on my side. He is an asset to my family. If half his claims are true, just dropping his name would get me out of paying taxes this year. It's good to have friends in high places.

"I haven't had that much fun discussing policy in years," he says with a chuckle. "You certainly know your politics."

"A girl has to stay current," I tell him. I'm winning him

over. He will be an ally for my family in the years to come. It's one step to making sure the Savio Family business lasts.

"Yes, this is true." He nods. "Will I be able to expect you at the next fundraiser?"

I look around the hotel. It's one of the nicer hotels outside of the city. The big ballroom is draped in red, white, and blue. There are stars and small flags decorating every table. It's gaudy, but nice.

"I would love to," I tell him. "Please make sure you let me know when it is."

As if I didn't get three invitations and a phone call for this one. Politicians will never forget you if you give them money, even once.

"Have you heard anything on the Michigan race?" I ask him. I'm prepared to donate more there as well. It's a cheap investment in making the senator a friend to the black family for life. Not only did I help his campaign, but I helped his party out as well.

"You haven't heard?" The senator looks surprised. "I thought you would have been the first to know. Finally, something I know that you don't!"

He looks pleased with himself for a moment.

"Now you have to tell me," I say, doing my best to flirt. However, a cold dread has started creeping up my spine.

"Senator Norwood has dropped out of the senate race," Grayson tells me. For a moment, I'm relieved. This is good news. Then he continues. "He's out of the senate race because he's announced he's going for the presidency."

In old-movies women faint when they hear bad news. I always thought it was an over exaggeration or a result of the constrictive gowns, but in this moment, I now understand it. I feel like I'm going to pass out.

Washington DC is only a three hour train ride. It's too close for comfort. My palms go sweaty just thinking about having Norwood that close to me. I'd rather he was in China. Or ten feet underground.

"Are you okay, Cara?" Senator Grayson asks me. "You look a little pale."

"As you know, I'm no friend to Senator Norwood. You said he's running for president?"

That man in charge of the country sounded like a dystopian future to me.

"Yes. It's not too unexpected, really." He shrugs. "It's a little early,

"I'll be happy to contribute to any candidate that runs against him," I quickly say. I will commit my entire inheritance to making sure he doesn't move to DC.

A predatory smile crosses the senator's face. "I was hoping you might say that."

"Why? Are you running?"

He laughs. "No. Not this cycle, though I might be tapped to be VP."

"So what will happen to all of my campaign contributions?" I ask with a coy smile.

He laughs and gives me a wink. "I think you'll find that every dollar is well spent. I always keep my constituents in mind."

"I'm glad to hear that," I say. "Will you let me know if you hear anything on Norwood's presidential campaign?"

"Of course." He glances around, making sure no one is listening to our conversation. "And if you happen to hear anything that might help discredit that campaign, I'd be very interested to know that as well. Anything you hear through your channels. I'm sure mattress sales have some interesting information."

I raise my eyebrows. At least now I'm sure Senator Grayson knows that my business isn't exactly mattress sales.

"If I learn anything, you'll be the first to know," I promise.

I wish I had something that could destroy Norwood. I would give my left foot to have something that would ruin his life the way he ruined mine.

"I'd appreciate that." He gives me a smile. "If you'll excuse me, I need to make the rounds."

"Of course." I smile and bob my head. There are lots of other wealthy benefactors for him to schmooze. The benefit of money being in politics these days is that I can buy it.

I'm tired. I've been tired all week. I wonder if I'm getting sick. I turn down a second glass of champagne. I've done my job. I've rubbed elbows with the people who are or will soon be powerful. It's time for me to go home and rest.

a knock on my door wakes me. It's still dark outside, but this late in the year it's practically dark until noon anyway. I climb out of my cocoon of blankets and pad over to the door to find Dante waiting for me.

Seeing him makes my heart do flip-flops. I'm glad my family picked him. This is a match that is good on paper and in real life.

"What are you doing here?" I ask, going up on my tiptoes to kiss him. His cheek is cold and there is snow in his dark hair.

"I was in the neighborhood," he replies, holding out a Styrofoam container. "I brought you some breakfast."

I giggle, taking it in my hands. I can already smell the delicious scent of french toast inside.

"You sure know how to spoil a girl," I say, grinning as I bring the container to the table and set it down. "Thank you."

He grins. It's boyish and heartwarming. I love it. I love the way his eyes sparkle. I brush the snow from his hair, my eyes going to his. His eyes are warm and brown, wrapping me up with heat.

I go up on my toes again and kiss his perfect lips. Suddenly, I don't care about breakfast anymore. I'm a different kind of hungry. I'm hungry for Dante.

I deepen our kiss, tracing the curve of his upper lip with my tongue and nibbling on his lower lip once I'm done. Kissing him is like getting drunk. I feel lightheaded and wonderful when his lips are on mine, and I never want to stop. I want to kiss him until the world ends.

"Vesper," he whispers. I love the deep, rumbling way he says my name. Like he's breathless to have me. Goosebumps pop up all over my skin, but they're not from the cold. Even though I'm only wearing a baggy, over-sized *I <3 NY* t-shirt and panties, I'm not even close to cold. I love that Dante wants me. Me. Not the escort, the girl that he's just paying to be what he wants. He just wants me.

My body is responding to the way he's kissing me. I know the instant he does anything more than just kiss me, my whole body is going to light up in flame. I'm so hot for him, I'm afraid I'm going to melt.

His hands tangle in my messy hair, pulling me further to him, and pressing his mouth harder against mine. I can't break free of his grasp, not that I want to. He's in complete control, but I know he isn't going to hurt me.

He's dangerous. I know this. One doesn't become a crime boss without being deadly. I know I've made my own grisly choices. Things that keep monsters awake in the night. It's all a matter of perspective. I keep my family safe. He keeps his family safe. Soon, we'll be family to each other.

My lust warped brain doesn't want to think about that though. I want to think about him filling me. I want to think about how are bodies are going to join and the look of pure ecstasy that fills Dante's face when he enters me for the first time. Just thinking about how his body reacts to mine has my temperature rising.

He pushes me to the bedroom and I willingly stumble along. The room is still blissfully dark with the curtains pulled, and I feel my way to the bed. The back of my knees hit first and I lay back with Dante's weight following me.

He runs his hands along my arms, drawing them up over my head and then pinning them to the bed. I arch my hips into his, pleased with the way he thrusts back. He wants me. One of Dante's hands stays on my wrists, keeping me in place, while the other goes to my thigh. His fingers caress the delicate, smooth skin of my thigh for a moment, then slowly move upward, inching my shirt along with his hand. Up over my hip, up my ribs, up to my breast. I love the way his hands feel against my skin. He's so strong and confident.

Slowly, he caresses the soft swell of my breast. Electric tingles of want explode out from his touch and travel straight to the V between my legs. He pinches my nipple and it puckers tight in his grip. He groans slightly and I buck my hips up to the sound.

I want him so bad. Every inch of my skin craves his touch. Every nerve is singing his name. I need him to fill me, to make me whole.

Dante stands up, turning to watch me as he takes off his jacket and starts to unbutton his shirt. His eyes are practically glowing in the dark with want. They never leave me. I am the center of his universe.

"You are so beautiful," he murmurs. I love the way his lips move. "Perfect."

Dante is all muscles and testosterone. I can't help but stare at the male perfection in front of me. I lick my lips in anticipation. I want to taste his skin. He grins, watching me, and slowly undoes his belt. His movements are sensual and teasing.

"Touch yourself," he commands. My hands fly to my panties without having to be told again. The thin, lacy fabric is already damp with my excitement. Dante's eyes flick to my fingers. "Take them off."

I pause for a moment and he holds perfectly still, his pant button halfway out of the hole. He's waiting for me. I have to do what he says for him to keep undressing. I quickly comply, wriggling out of my panties and throwing them to the floor. I'm back in position on the bed, angled so that he can see me.

Dante finishes undoing the button on his pants. His fingers hold the zipper to his fly, but he stops there. "Shirt, too," he says.

I grin, and pull my shirt up and over my head. I'm naked in front of him and reveling in the way his pupils dilate when he looks at me.

"Keep touching yourself," he reminds me, pulling his pants down just enough for me to see the bulge of his desire through his fly. He waits to go further until I comply.

My fingers swirl into pleasure and I gasp. I imagine it's his fingers instead of my own as he lowers his pants. I can see the outline of his erection through the fabric of his underwear. He's hard and ready for me. I've never wanted anyone as badly as I want him. I close my eyes for a moment as I slide two fingers into my damp heat. It's a pale substitute for what I really want, but it still makes my hips arch up.

"Harder," he commands. I open my eyes to see him staring at my fingers. He wets his lips and his hand twitches like he wants to do it himself, but he's holding back. Watching. I pump my fingers in and out, moaning at the increase in pressure building in my core.

Dante strips the last of his clothing and kneels on the bed. His hand reaches for mine, and before I can thrust it into me again, he takes it and puts my wet fingers in his mouth. The difference of heat and the light suction of his tongue make me shiver.

"Delicious," he whispers. His voice is rough, like he can barely contain the animal within him trying to get out. He keeps sucking on my fingers as he slides his own between my legs to continue my pleasure. I gasp as he pushes past his knuckles, going deep and feeling every inch of me with his fingertips.

"Come for me." He pushes deeper. "I want to feel it."

My hands go to my nipples, pinching and teasing them into tight buds of sensation as he beckons my body to orgasm with his fingers. He's fucking me with his fingers and I can't help but moan. He's rough but gentle at the same time, pushing my body to explode.

Dante kisses my thigh, his unshaven face scratching the tender skin slightly. His tongue traces up the curve of my leg, up to the rise of my hip bone where he bites down. It's not hard, but it's enough sensation to overwhelm me. It's all I need to skitter over the edge. I succumb to pleasure, to his touch, and to him. I lose control of my body as it contracts and writhes around Dante's fingers.

I wasn't expecting an orgasm that powerful, but something about having Dante watch me makes it so much better. So much hotter. More intense and personal.

As I wind down, he removes his fingers. "My turn," he says, sensually licking the fingers that had just been inside me. "So sweet, Vesper. So sweet."

Before I've even finished coming down from the high of my orgasm, he's at my entrance. I want him in me, I need him in me. Without him, I don't feel complete. I arch and writhe, trying to pull him inside of me, but he just hovers on the edge, teasing me with his control.

Slowly, more slowly than I can tolerate, he pushes in. I can't make him go faster or slower, no matter how much I struggle for more. I want to feel him run me through and complete me, but he takes his time. Finally, when he is enveloped to the hilt, I am content.

He starts to pump his hips, using his athletic ass to rail into me. It starts gentle, but he is in control and his lust is quickly eroding his will to stay slow. I cry out in pleasure, and he stuffs his fingers into my mouth. I can still taste my own ecstasy on his fingers. I suck, wanting as much of him in me as I can take.

"On your hands and knees," he growls, pulling back. His absence is like a knife wound. I need to have the gape filled or I'm afraid I'll die. I need his body like I need oxygen.

I willingly flip over and rise up on all fours. With a grin back at him, I wave my ass from side to side, inviting him to take me.

His hand comes down in a spank I wasn't expecting. I yelp and jump, but he just grabs my hips. With a gentleness that I don't expect, he rubs the red hand print on my ass. The soft caress is almost painful against the angry, reddened skin. I want more.

"Do it again," I request, biting my lip. His lips twitch and his hand comes down on the same spot. Pain and lust spike through me and I arch my back, my ass in the air like a cat in heat. I love the way the pleasure and pain mingle and dance through my body.

He slams his hips into me, filling me so completely I can barely stand it. My fingers pull at the sheets and I scream his name into the pillow. I'm loosing my sense of reality to his animalistic thrusts and strength. I love the noises, the grunts and heavy breathing, coming from behind me.

He spanks me again, pain filling the abused skin and I scream with wanton need. I can't hold back the tide of pleasure as he thrusts his hips into mine. I come hard on him. Every muscle in my body, every nerve, every fiber of my being tightens to pull him into me, begging his body to join mine in heaven.

I forget to breathe. The pleasure is so intense I can barely move. I hover between ultimate fulfillment and a lust for more. I know I will want this again and again. And that only Dante can give this to me. This level of pleasure is Dante's trademark.

"Fuck, fuck, fuck..." I hear him groan, his head falling back as my body massages his. His hands are on my hips as he dives into me. "You're so fucking tight..."

He can't stop. I can feel the change in his grip on my hips, the way his hips press that much harder, even the tone of his voice and the ragged edge to his breathing. I don't want him to hold back. I want him to join me in this amazing world of pleasure the two of us have created. I feel him release, his whole body shuddering and freezing with release. Our bodies merge and mingle.

I can't believe how good this is. Or how badly I had wanted him. His pumps are slow and sensual now, as the two of us enjoy the heightened nerves and senses that can only come with release.

I have never craved another human being like I crave Dante. Even after the best orgasm of my life, I still want more. I'm sure I'll never want anything else but Dante.

I ache for more, even as he pulls away and collapses on the bed beside me. He's breathing hard and fast, with a sheen of sweat coating his perfectly sculpted chest.

This is how every day should start, I think to myself. I could get used to this. I could start my days out with amazing sex and end them the same way.

I lay still on the bed, just feeling my heartbeat slowly return to normal. Dante has the ability to make me feel. That both frightens me and comforts me. If I don't choose him, I'm afraid no one will ever make me feel this way again. I look into his eyes and see everything I could want there. A future. My heart thrills and I decide to throw caution to the winds. Dante won't fail me. His mother's threat are just empty words.

My mother is gone. There is no bringing her back. She would want me to be happy. I am happy with Dante. Revenge isn't for the dead. It's for the living. It's a way to cope with grief so strong that we can't handle it all at once. We have to concentrate on hating something just so that our hearts don't shatter.

Victoria can keep her information. She can burn it, give it to Norwood, or print it in the New York Times. It's not a threat to me anymore. I'm at peace. I still ache to avenge my mother, but not at the price of loosing Dante. Not if I lose the way I feel right now.

And right now, I feel happy.

CHAPTER 19

"Come to our house," Aunt Sophia says on the phone. "Your uncle wants to see you. I want to see you. I made your favorite."

"You made chicken parmigiana?" My mouth starts to water.

"From scratch," Aunt Sophia tempts me.

"I'll be there," I promise. There is little that I wouldn't do for real home cooked food. Especially food made by my aunt. That woman could have been a chef in a different life.

Ethan picks me up and drives me out to the burbs. My aunt and uncle have a comfortable house with a large backyard. They own a beach house out on Cape Cod, but other than some expensive trips, they keep the extent of their wealth to themselves.

Uncle Tony says that doing that and paying our fair share of taxes will keep the feds off our backs. Considering it's worked so well and that he has friends in the IRS now, I believe him.

"Dinner's almost ready," Aunt Sophia says as I walk in. "Go wash your hands. You too, Ethan."

Ethan nods a "yes, ma'am" and goes to the bathroom. He always eats with us if he drives me. Once he tried to sit out in the car while we ate and my aunt flipped her lid. If there's food, then everyone eats in her world. We don't leave people hungry.

I go to the kitchen and wash my hands there. "Can I help?"

My aunt points to the cutting board where salad things are waiting to be chopped. I smile. She's had that ready for me since I was a kid. Making the salad has always been my job. I pick up the knife and quickly begin chopping.

"I wanted to tell you that you did good the other day," she says, opening the oven and checking on her chicken. "I heard Senator Grayson is very pleased with you."

I smile a little. "Thank you, Aunt Sophia."

She turns. Her dark hair is up in a bun, but I can see there is a lot more gray in it than there used to be. She has a stern face where I remember my mother's being softer.

"You look so like your mother," she says softly. A sad smile crosses her face. "Sometimes, I see her in you. I see her energy. Her joy in things."

"I miss her." I stop cutting vegetables for a moment.

My aunt wraps her arms around me. "Me too. That evil man took her away from us too soon."

I know she's talking about Norwood. When my mother died, my uncle tried everything to connect her death with Norwood. Nothing ever stuck. Yet, somehow, the coroner that ruled my mother's death an accident somehow was able to afford a brand new Porsche.

He covered it up, but we've never been able to prove it. My whole family knows. It's just something we've come to accept now. Well, except me.

She sighs and lets me go. "Your uncle will be hungry. Hurry up with that salad."

I chuckle, but finish quickly. We always make a salad, but my uncle never eats it. He eats meat and potatoes only.

The table is just as I remember from my teenage years. It's a heavy wooden table with heavy wooden chairs. My uncle sits at the head of the table with my aunt next to him. Uncle Tony is discussing something with Ethan. They both have low voices, so I assume it's something to do with business.

My uncle smiles as I enter the room. "Cara."

I go over and kiss his cheek. I still see him as the man who came to rescue me when I was twelve years old. He's twenty pounds heavier and lost most of his hair, but to me he is still tall and strong.

"Hi, Uncle Tony."

"I'm so glad your aunt was able to convince you to come to dinner tonight," he tells me. "It's been too long since you've come over."

I help my aunt bring food to the table. Old gender traditions die hard.

"I know. I've been busy with work," I reply, setting down the mashed potatoes down near Uncle Tony. They're his favorite.

A proud smile tugs on the edges of his lips, but he stays stern. "I know. I heard you've made a friend in a Senator Grayson?"

I nod, sitting down at my place. "He's friends with Chief O'Brien. They are both very happy to have our campaign contributions."

The small proud smile twitch goes again. "I'm so glad you've taken so well to the business."

"I like it," I tell him. "I have some ideas I want to run past you. With the addition of the Russos, we have some new opportunities."

The smile comes full on this time. "Of course." The smile disappears for a moment. "Are you happy with him?"

My chest warms with his concern. He isn't one to talk much of feelings.

"I like him," I tell him honestly. "It's a good match. And it's good for business. So, yes. I'm happy."

My uncle takes a deep breath and relaxes. He must have been worried about me. Despite the business, he sees me as his daughter. He and my aunt officially adopted me. Just because business is important, it doesn't trump family.

"Ethan? Do you need anything?" my aunt asks.

"I'm good," he says. Short and blunt as always. I shake my head and take a serving of my aunt's chicken.

Our conversation moves to other things. My uncle is smiling now that he knows I'm happy. I feel safe here. My family keeps me safe. The future is bright.

My uncle's phone rings. He glares at it, but answers since it's his work phone.

"Go." His voice is sharp. He doesn't like being interrupted during dinner. He nods, listening to the caller. "Now? I'll send her."

He hangs up the phone.

"Who was that?" Aunt Sophia asks. We're almost done with dinner.

"It was the senator," Uncle Tony says. He shakes his head. "He wants to meet with Cara. It's important. A business opportunity."

Another proud smile fills his face. It's rare for me to get two in one night. I can barely remember the last time I had even just one. This seems to be my night.

"You'll go meet with him," he tells me. It's a combination of question and statement. I have the choice to not go.

"Of course I'll meet with him," I quickly say. I want that proud smile again. I want him to know that I can take care of the family business. I want him to know that he's made a good choice in me. That all these years of training me and teaching me were worth the effort.

I want him to be proud of me.

"Bring Ethan," my aunt says. She starts picking up dishes. I stand up to help. "No, Cara. You have an important meeting to go to."

I stand there for a moment at a loss. It's always been my job to help with dishes. The fact that I don't means that I'm really moving up in the world. I'm important.

"Ethan, you ready?" I ask. He nods and stands, thanking my aunt and uncle for their hospitality.

My uncle gives me a nod. I'm an equal now. I'm going to head the organization. I'm a little nervous, but right now, I'm bursting with pride.

I am truly a mob boss. I am powerful.

CHAPTER 20

"Are you sure this is right, Ethan?" I ask, looking out my window at the creepy, abandoned looking office building. There are broken windows and several burnt out streetlights. It doesn't exactly look like a great place to discuss campaign finances.

"Yes." Ethan holds up the card and shrugs. "You want me to come in with you?"

I want to say yes. But, if I'm going to head up this organization, I can't have my body guard all the time. Especially if I'm discussing slightly illegal campaign issues with a sitting senator. It's better I do this alone.

"I think I should go in alone," I say. I don't like the way my stomach twists when I say it. It's a bad omen, but it's too late to turn back now.

"I'll be right out here if you need anything."

A flutter of worry bubbles up in my stomach. Ethan will be a long way away if anything goes wrong tonight. I tell myself I've had plenty of self-defense lessons. I'll be fine.

I step out into the night. Old snow crunches under my feet as I leave the safety and warmth of Ethan's car and go into the building. The inside isn't much better than the outside. The heat's obviously been turned off for the night but at least the stairwell is well lit. I'll be able to find Suite 302 without too much trouble.

I have to walk the full length of the building and as far away from Ethan as I can get without actually leaving the premises to find the door I'm looking for. I stand there nervously for a moment before opening it. Something in my gut tells me to run. Tells me that I need to get back to Ethan as quickly as possible and never look back.

But that would mean admitting I was scared. That would be admitting defeat.

So I open the door.

The light is off in the room. It makes the silhouette of the man against the window that much more striking. For a moment, I think it's Dante, that this whole thing is his elaborate attempt to tease me. That would make sense. It makes me smile, and I step forward, hearing the door close behind me.

"Dante?"

The man turns from the window and the lights flicker on.

It is definitely not Dante. In fact, it's the last person in the entire world that I want to see.

"Hello, Cara."

Raw fear steals my voice and I step back. This is the voice I hear in my nightmares.

"No..." I whisper, my limbs not responding to my thoughts anymore. "No..."

"That's no way to greet an old friend," he says, frowning slightly.

"What are you doing here?" I whisper, grabbing at the doorknob, desperate to get away, but it's locked behind me. Someone must have locked it when it shut. I'm trapped in the room with him. With John Norwood, the man who ruined my life and haunts my nightmares. I keep trying the door, even though I know it's futile.

"I'm here to see you." He moves forward, stepping further into the light of the room. He's the same height as Dante, but that's the last similarity between them.

Norwood has thin blonde hair where Dante's is luxurious and dark, a paunch in his stomach where Dante is all muscle, and age where Dante is young. But it's the eyes that are the real difference between them. Dante's are dark and wild, but with a kindness and warmth that keeps them bright. John Norwood's are brown, but evil and cold. There is no warmth or charm, no redemption to the darkness residing underneath. They are flat, like a shark's.

The eyes are so emotionless that I am surprised that my mother ever saw love in them.

In my initial terror, he looked exactly the way I remembered him, but a second look reveals the changes. On the edges of my vision I catch glimpses of the bald patch covered by a bad comb-over, and the weight around his middle. There are more wrinkles around his mouth and less strength to his shoulders. However, for the most part, I still see him as the man he was over a decade ago. My mind is unable to see anything but the man who took my mother from me.

Norwood reaches out and strokes my cheek with his fingertip. The motion is soft and gentle, but it spurs my panic. I press hard into the door, wishing I could just pass through it like a ghost. I wish I were a ghost. It would be better than being trapped here with him.

His hand traces the curve of my face, down to my throat, caressing me softly. Without warning, his fingers tighten around the delicate base of my throat, squeezing just hard enough to make the primal fear of suffocation very real.

"Did you think you could hide from me, Cara?" he growls, bringing his face close to mine. His breath stinks of mints and cigarette smoke. "Did you think I wouldn't find you? That you would be safe here?"

I squirm, trying to get away. When I was younger, he was gentle with me, but I saw the marks he left on my mother. I saw the bruises. I went with her to the doctor's appointments where she said she tripped. I knew what evil he was capable of.

"So pretty, just like your mother. You whimper just like her too, you know." He smiles a cold smile. "I wonder if you'll look just as pretty stretched out on the road."

I decide right there that I'm going to kill him, even if it's the last thing I ever do.

Norwood laughs at my struggles, tightening his grip. My vision is fading and my limbs won't move the way I want them too. He waits until my vision is just a tiny pinprick of light before releasing me. I fall to the ground, shaking and gasping for air.

"I'll kill you, you bastard!" I screech, my throat raw from his hand.

"It's good to see you have your mother's fire," he says with a chuckle. He squats down in front of me. His disgusting eyes are the only objects that aren't fuzzy in my world. "I was afraid you would have lost it having the mob protect you at every turn. I'm glad to see your mother passed that on to you."

"Don't you talk about her," I growl. Speaking hurts my throat.

He laughs in my face. The smell of covered-up cigarette smoke makes me nauseous.

"She had fire too, you know. It's why I was so angry when she said she was leaving me. She was so delicious. That skin. Those delicate hands..."

I look up at him and his mouth curves into a cruel smile.

He's enjoying tormenting me with this. He's found a weak spot in my armor and he's pressing it as hard as he can.

"Why did you have to ruin things? I could have been a good father to you," he says. His voice is soothing and he's put his face into something that looks paternal and caring. It's a mask and I know I can't trust it, but it's hard not too when he looks at me like that. I know that that mask is why he's so successful in politics. People trust him.

"What do you want from me?" I ask, staggering to my feet. I can see again, though I'm still having trouble catching my breath.

"Oh, lots of things."

"I'll get you what you want. You want campaign money? You can have it," I tell him. "I have connections."

"I know you do, but that's not what I need."

I swallow hard. This is going to be bad. This night is not going to end well.

"You ran from me, Cara. You denied me, you defied me, and you made me come looking for you. I'm not pleased, Cara. Not pleased at all." He steps toward me and I shrink back as much as possible.

"I'm not my mother," I whisper. "You killed her."

"You have no proof." He shrugs. "But, you are the same as her. Just seeing you fills me with nostalgia. I hear you play piano almost as well as she did."

"I don't play at all," I lie. I look around the room, searching for an escape. I can't find one. Panic flutters at the bottom of my ribs and it's taking everything I have not to lose my calm.

"Oh, yes you do. Your favorite is Clair de Lune. You play it almost as well as your mother, but you always off on the arpeggios. You should work on your left hand more."

My eyes go wide. I've never played in public. I've only

ever played in my home and there is no way he should know that I even play it, let alone which hand is struggling.

"You see, Cara, you never escaped me. I knew where you were all along because you belong to me. Your mother was mine and now you're mine." His lips curve up in a cruel smile.

I hate the way he says my name. It makes my skin crawl and I wish he would call me anything else.

"Why'd you wait ten years?" I ask. I'm proud that my voice doesn't crack. I feel like I'm made of cracks and at any moment, I'll shatter into a million pieces.

"I was busy." He shrugs as if I can be replaced if he desires. "You aren't my only plaything. I wanted to see what you would do on your own, and frankly, I'm rather disappointed. Though, what should I have expected of trailer-trash in the first place?"

"Fuck you," I lash out. I'm surprised that his disappointment still hurts and sick that I still have the innate desire to seek his approval. Somehow, I still see him as a father figure from dating my mother.

His hand moves faster than I remember and I suddenly see stars. The pain of his slap comes only a little bit after, burning and tingling across my cheek. In one smooth motion, he grips my throat again. He squeezes and it hurts more this time. The bruises are already aching.

I see an opportunity and bring my knee up as hard as I can, hoping to catch him off guard. He bats my knee away with his leg as if it's nothing and shakes his head.

"No, no little Cara," he whispers, sounding like a doting father chastising a petulant child. "You're mine. You need to learn your place."

I scream, loosing all the power in my lungs in a plea for help. I pray that Ethan hears me, that someone-- anyone-- comes to my rescue. He slams my head against the door. Red blurs my vision and I feel sick to my stomach. I wish I would just black out.

"Go ahead and scream again," he dares me. He pushes his body against mine and I can feel his superior strength as I struggle. "This place is deserted. No one is going to help you."

My next scream dies in my throat and I let out a weak whimper instead. Mr. Norwood's eyes burn with darkness. There is no warmth to them. No chance of pity or redemption. The only thing I can see is hate and pain.

"Fuck you," I whisper. There's much less strength to my words this time, but I am determined to fight him. I'm not the same girl I was ten years ago.

"That won't do, Cara," he says, using my name like a leash to hold me against my will. He tucks a strand of hair behind my ear. The gentle motion is a strange contradiction to the heartlessness he's shown me. "I'm going to have to break you. I will destroy everything you hold dear if you fight me."

I stubbornly stick my chin out. "I'll stop you."

He slaps me again and stars dance across my vision.

"Your Savio family crime syndicate?" He scoffs. "They only think you're safe. They let you come to this meeting. What good protectors they are."

"I have other ways," I hiss. This isn't my family's fault. This is mine. I should have brought Ethan. I'll never make this mistake again.

"You mean you'll get your precious Dante to stop me?" He laughs and the sound makes me shiver. "Go ahead and try it. I'll destroy him. I own the world he operates in. He can't save you. No one can."

I set my jaw. I'm not going to let fear overcome me. He's bluffing. There's no way he's that powerful. Dante won't fail me.

A slow, sinister grin crosses Mr. Norwood's face. It's a

thing of nightmares. "You are so like your mother, Cara. I should have come for you earlier."

I close my eyes as he winds up his hand again. Stars aren't the right word for the tiny floating lights that fill my vision.

Be strong. You can survive this. You can survive anything, I tell myself. I cling to those words as he hits me again. And again. And again.

Be strong.

CHAPTER 21

I stumble out of the building and out into the cold. I hate the cold, but at least I'm free.

My clothing is torn beyond saving and I'm bleeding from my lip and at least one cut above my eye. I'm fairly sure the back of my head is bleeding, but I don't dare stop to try and find out. I have to get away from him. At least all he did was hit me.

"Cara?" Ethan calls, closing the car door behind him and hurrying across the snow. I must look like a disaster for him to have left the car. I certainly feel like a disaster. He catches me just as my legs give out. He's so warm, but all I can think about is how I'm getting blood on his suit.

He cradles me close and runs to the car. I didn't know he was that strong, but I feel safe now that I have Ethan here. Ethan won't let Mr. Norwood hurt me. He would have stopped Mr. Norwood if he had known.

"You need a doctor," Ethan says quietly, his eyes going to the gash above my eye. Worry darkens his face as he tucks me into the car and pulls the remnants of my dress up around my shoulder. I think of telling him no. I hate doctors.

But everything hurts and blood is trickling down my face. I don't want a scar. I nod weakly, pain spiking the motion.

Ethan's brows knit. His concern for me is only growing, and if anything that unsettles me more than the blood on my face. He runs to the driver's seat and peels out of the parking lot. The car surges with power as he pushes it as fast as he can.

I close my eyes. I'm tired straight through my bones. I haven't been this exhausted in a long, long time. I don't know how my mother put up with it for as long as she did.

Probably fear of something worse.

I feel like I've only blinked, but when I open my eyes, I see the bright lights of an urgent care. I'm glad he brought me here instead of a hospital. Ethan is opening the door, but I don't have the strength to stand. He picks me up and carries me inside like I'm a small child. I rest my head against his shoulder, content to be small for a moment.

The waiting room is empty and a nurse takes one look at me and runs for a doctor. I only notice that Ethan has set me down on a gurney because I'm suddenly cold without him holding me.

Ethan glances at the doctor running in our direction. "I need to call Tony. Are you okay by yourself?" His voice is thick with guilt. He thinks he has failed me even though Mr. Norwood set him up to fail.

"This isn't your fault, Ethan." I mean it. I was the one who told him to stay in the car. I was the one who wanted to look important. If I'd just let him do his job, Ethan wouldn't have that guilty look plastered on his face.

"I'll be fine, Ethan," I tell him as the doctor reaches us. "Look, the doctor's here. I'll be okay." I try to smile, but the movement makes me wince with pain instead.

Ethan hesitates for a moment before moving to let the doctor poke and prod. The doctor closes the thin blue curtain behind him and looks me over. I answer his questions as best I can, telling him what hurts and what doesn't. I tell him that I was mugged.

Through a crack in the curtain I can see Ethan on the phone. His face is grim and determined. I can see him take a deep breath before picking it back up again.

"Did the man who brought you here do this to you?" the doctor asks. His face is worried and I know he saw Ethan slam the phone as well.

"Ethan?" I shake my head, ignoring the pain that it causes. "I told you I was mugged. Ethan would never have allowed this to happen if he had been there. He keeps me safe."

The doctor nods, not fully believing me. To be honest, I'd have a hard time believing the beaten up girl with the violent man bringing her in too. "Would you like to file a report? I'd recommend it."

I almost laugh. What would I report? That the esteemed political powerhouse John Norwood beat me? I'd be dead in two seconds. John Norwood is willing to kill. "No. No report."

"If you change your mind, let me know." The doctor looks unconvinced, but isn't going to argue with me. "We'll take you for x-rays once we get that cut stitched up. Regardless of what we find, I'm going to prescribe a mild pain killer and a sedative so you can get some sleep tonight. I'm also prescribing you an antibiotic. That cut on your cheek looks nasty, and I'd rather it not become infected. Check with the pharmacist to see if this will affect any other medication you're on."

I nod, not really paying attention.

"Is there any possibility you could be pregnant?" the doctor asks.

I almost say no, but then I think back. My period should have started today. "I'm not sure," I say instead.

"We'll do a pregnancy test before the x-rays," he says. I watch him leave. I relish the quiet silence once he leaves. I want to be alone. If I close my eyes and hold perfectly still, I can almost pretend that nothing happened. That it was all just a bad dream. And that's all I want it to be.

~

"Vesper?"

John Norwood is here for me, I think as I startle awake. I claw at the thin sheet, desperate to pull it around me and hid until I realize that Mr. Norwood wouldn't call me Vesper. I take a deep breath to slow the pounding of my heart, but I'm surprised that I was able to sleep at all.

The light turns on and the curtain opens. It's Dante, not Norwood. I'm safe. He closes the curtain behind him.

Dante's eyes take in the bruises and bandages and anger curls the edges of his mouth. As his gaze goes to mine, he sees the fear still lingering in the corners of my eyes. Concern fills his eyes and anger flashes that someone would do this to me.

He's dangerous with that look.

Dante sits carefully on the edge of my bed, the anger gone from his eyes as quickly as it came. He leans forward and carefully kisses my hairline. It's the one place on my entire body that doesn't hurt and I'm glad he's the one that found it.

"What happened?" he asks. His voice is low and soothing.

"I thought I was meeting Senator Grayson," I tell him. "I told Ethan to stay in the car. I didn't want to spook him. I wanted to prove that I could be a boss on my own."

Shame heats my cheeks. It was such a stupid thing to do. I don't even really know why I did it. It just seemed right at the time.

"It wasn't Grayson." I am an idiot. I should have suspected

something. I should have fought back harder. I should have done a lot of things differently.

Dante growls. "I'll kill him."

Cold fire burns in his blue eyes. Dante is my protector. He will make this right. He won't let this go unpunished. Dante will make sure I'm safe. I know this. The first tear of the night slides down my cheek, stinging the angry skin as it falls.

"I'd like that," I whisper. I mean it. "It was John Norwood. The man I think killed my mother."

"He's a dead man," Dante assures me. I fold into his arms, feeling momentarily safe against his strong chest. I'm going to call Mr. Norwood's bluff. Dante is going to kill him and I'll finally be free.

What if it's not a bluff? The voice asks, but I ignore it.

"Let me take you home," Dante says.

I nod, suddenly anxious to be home with my own things instead of trapped by wires and IVs. Dante opens the curtain and I see Ethan standing guard. Dante nods to him and Ethan goes to pick up my meager belongings from the plastic chair next to the gurney as Dante picks me up.

Together, my two protectors take me home.

CHAPTER 22

Wake in my own bed, and for a moment, I'm sure
that the whole night was just a bad dream. Then I
hear Dante yelling in the other room and I frown. The frown
sends a streak of pain across my face and I sigh, knowing
that it wasn't just a nightmare.

I sit up slowly. Luckily, all the x-rays came back negative.
They seemed strangely concerned with having me cover my
torso with the lead apron, but I had been to tired to care. A
minor concussion, fourteen stitches on my face and twelve
on the back of my head, and a full suite of bruises. The
emotional trauma was just as bad. My pride is bruised as
much as my body.

I see a voicemail on my phone.

"Ms. Savio. This is the doctor from last night. I need to
speak with you when you get a chance. Please call me at this
number."

I frown a little. I hope they didn't find anything else
wrong with my labs and tests after I left. I'd call them once I
had some food.

I slither out of bed, trying to move as little as possible. I go to the living room to find Dante staring out the window, his fist balled up tight against the glass. He turns as he hears the bedroom door.

"Did I wake you?" He looks frustrated and runs a hand through his dark hair. "I'm sorry."

"I just need some coffee." I smile, moving my expression slowly to keep the pain away, and move closer to him. "You look like I feel. What's wrong?"

"Nothing you need to worry about." Dante just shakes his head and then forces a smile. "Would you like me to order you some breakfast?"

"Just coffee right now," I tell him. My stomach is clenched tight with stress. If Dante's worried, then I'm worried. I touch his arm, trying to get him to open up to me. "You can tell me. Otherwise, I'll just worry."

His smile stays wooden, but he leans forward and kisses my forehead. "Just business. Three new lawsuits, a broken contract, and to top it all off-" he pauses and holds up his phone for effect, "a reporter from the Times is calling to ask me about some rather concerning allegations. The police have already called me twice, and it's not even noon yet."

"That's terrible." I bite my lip. I don't like the way this sounds. He shrugs and goes to the kitchen and pours me a cup of coffee.

"It's strange, really," Dante muses, adding a little sugar to the black liquid for me.

"How bad is it?" I ask, following him to the warm kitchen counter.

"Bad." He frowns and hands me the cup of coffee. "But I don't want you to worry."

I kiss him on the cheek and then take a sip of my coffee. It's sweet and perfect. Just like him. "How about I worry just a little bit? So you don't have to quite as much."

He grins and kisses my head again. "I want you to know,

I'm taking care of your problem. It should be solved by the end of the week. I can make it sooner if you want. The price isn't a problem."

For once, I question my Aunt's lack of desire to use hired killers. In this situation, it feels justified.

"Thank you." I mean it. I set my coffee down and smile up at him. A weight I didn't know was there lifts from my shoulders. I'm going to be free. Free of the monster that has haunted my dreams for so long. Really free. My mother avenged. And it's all because of Dante.

I kiss him. It starts sweet, but my hormones start to take over. I need him, more than just emotionally. I need to show Dante how much he means to me. How grateful I am that he's saving me.

I don't mean for it to become sexual, but what he is doing for me means so much, and I don't know any other way to thank him. I know how to show gratitude with my body, not my words. I need to show him.

He kisses me back until he remembers I'm injured.

"Vesper," he says, pulling away . His hands are tangled in my hair. "I don't want to hurt you."

"Then be gentle," I tell him, grazing my lips against his. "But I need you. I need to show you how much this means to me."

I look up at him. He's so beautiful. Strong. Young. Safe. I'm safe with him.

He presses his lips against mine, his teeth nibbling on my lower lip as his tongue invades my mouth. He tastes sweet, like heaven.

His hands go to my hips. He makes sure that he doesn't hurt me. He kisses my lips, but then moves his mouth to my throat, down to my collar bone and then to the collar of my nightshirt. A low, happy noise of pleasure is the only sound I can make as he lifts my shirt and hooks his fingers around my panties and pulls. They slide off my legs easy and once I'm free of them, his hands are on my waist again.

With wonderful ease, he picks me up and sets me on the kitchen counter. The granite is cold on my bare butt, but everything else about me is heating up. The fires of lust are burning brightly deep in my belly. My body is craving more.

Dante puts his hands on my knees and spreads them wide. He goes to his knees, kissing up from my feet. He is so careful it makes me want to cry. From my feet, up my shins, up to my thighs, he avoids every bruise and scrape, concentrating on kissing only the skin that won't hurt at his touch. By the time he reaches the top of my legs, I'm panting with want.

His beautiful dark eyes flash up to mine once before he lowers his head and presses his tongue against my sweet spot. I whimper with pleasure, tangling my hands in his dark hair as he begins to work his magic. His tongue swirls and his lips suck and play with me in all the right ways.

My legs start to vibrate as I approach the precipice of my climax. All the stress of yesterday melts away under his careful ministrations. Mr. Norwood is going away and it's because of Dante. I'll be safe. No more fear.

I let myself go. Lights and colors fill my vision as my entire body clenches and rocks on ecstasy. This is what it feels like to be happy.

Slowly, once the colors fade, I open my eyes. Dante is staring up at me, watching me with those beautiful eyes of his. They are blue sapphires of adoration and care. His mouth curves upward slightly when our eyes connect. I can't help but smile back at him.

His hand grazes one of the large purple bruises on my thigh as he stands and I wince. I'm surprised that something so superficial can hurt so much, but the after-effects of my orgasm quickly diminish due to the sudden pain.

"Sorry," Dante apologizes, moving his hand to a different spot. I can't help it. I squirm slightly at his touch, afraid that he will accidentally hurt me again. "I won't hurt you," he says, putting his hand firmly on the counter where it won't do any harm.

I bite my lip and look up at him.

"Let me in, Vesper," he coaxes, putting his hands on my knees and carefully avoiding the bruises. I let him push. I want to let him in. I want to have him with me. I relax and he steps into the space between my legs.

He kisses me again. I close my eyes and focus on the way his soft lips feel against mine. The gentle scratch of his stubble on my cheek and how his masculine, wonderful scent is taking me away. I love how good he smells.

Dante's hand slides down from his kiss, gentle and feather soft as he searches for my breast. He cups the swell of my breast though my nightshirt, teasing my nipple with his thumb. He's so gentle and his kisses are so warm.

My hands go to his belt and I fumble with the button on his pants as he continues his kissing. He's hard and long already. My fingers wrap around his shaft. It's like steel covered with satin. Suddenly, everything within me needs him. A need so strong that I can barely remember to breath because of it overcomes me. I need him in me. Now.

I wrap my legs around his waist, positioning his swelling girth and then guiding him into me. My legs tighten, drawing him further in. I love the small gasp he makes as he enters me. It's pure pleasure. I want more of him. I want all of him.

Dante pumps his hips in and out in a slow, lazy motion. There is no urgency, not yet, to his motions. This is all about my pleasure and showing me that he cares. This is slow and loving, not fast and hard. This is what I need. But I want more.

I tighten my legs around him, pulling him deeper and arching my back to give him even more.

"Vesper..." he groans, his eyes rolling to the back of his head and his fingers tightening on the counter. "You have no idea what you do to me."

But I do. Because he does the same thing to me.

I put my hands on either side of his face and peer into his eyes. There's so much emotion there, yet so much youth. He is everything I want and shouldn't have. I don't deserve a love like his. He has so much potential that I almost feel guilty about marrying him and keeping him for myself. Almost.

"Don't hold back," I whisper, looking deeply into his dark eyes. "I want you. Please."

I squeeze my legs tighter, showing him what I mean in addition to the words. His pace quickens. Every thrust fills me with pleasure. I've forgotten the bruises and the pain for a moment. I'm lost on the pleasure he's giving me.

I watch with heavy lids as his brow furrows in concentrations, his motions becoming stronger and more insistent, until his eyes go wide. I feel the hot splash of his seed as he finds his release. It's like a gun going off and filling me with warmth and light. I draw him into me, pulling as much of his essence and strength into me as I can. I need him. I wish I could have a part of him inside of me like this forever.

"You drive me insane, Vesper," Dante gasps. His eyes hold nothing but innocent love for me.

"Right back at you, Bond." I grin and kiss his forehead. I can't believe how good I feel right now with him. "Thank you."

He waits until his breathing is back to normal before stepping back and leaving me aching for him again. I feel strangely full and empty at the same time.

I grab the roll of paper towels from beside me and hand him several before getting some for myself. I slide off the counter, wincing as I catch a sore spot on my way down. We clean up, stealing smiles and glances.

It takes me a minute to find my panties, but I put them back on. I'm suddenly very tired. I need a pain pill and some more sleep. Or caffeine.

I reach for my coffee and find that it's still warm, which makes me smile. I take a pain pill and the antibiotic. I have to remember to check my birth control prescription, but that is low on my list of priorities. Life is good right now.. When John Norwood is dead, I can have mornings like this every-day. Without the bruises. I feel the world opening up with possibilities for me and Dante without Norwood haunting my past.

My phone, the one I only use for emergencies, starts to ring on the counter. Dante answers, then frowns and holds the phone out to me. "It's for you."

I set down my coffee and take the phone with a bad feeling coming over me.

"I hear Mr. Russo is having a bad day."

Mr. Norwood's voice makes my knees give out and I drop into a chair. My heart is pounding and I'm glad the only thing in my stomach is a couple of sips of coffee because I'm fairly sure I'm going to be sick.

"You want his problems to stop? Reign in your dog and I'll let him survive this." I can hear the derision in Mr. Norwood's voice drip across every word like spilled blood. "You're mine, but I know how unhappy you'll be if anything bad happened to your young pet. Stop him from making a very stupid decision or the Feds will find his hit-man's receipts. He has some secrets I'm sure he'd rather not be shared."

"Why are you doing this?"

"Because it's fun. Oh, and if you say a word of any of this

to your little Dante-y, I'll have him killed. You know I can make it look like an accident."

My mouth is dry as the line goes dead. All my happy, good feelings are gone. I'm empty and suddenly cold.

I wasn't free. I would never be free. I am doomed.

I drop more than set the phone down, but I twist my face into something that doesn't look like terror before I turn back to face Dante.

"Who was it?" he asks, pouring himself a cup of coffee.

"My hair stylist just confirming an appointment." Lying to him is surprisingly easy. I stand up and go to him. I need to protect him from this. Mr. Norwood wasn't bluffing. "Dante, I've been thinking. I don't want you to take care of Norwood. Stop whatever it is that you have planned. I've changed my mind."

Dante frowns, confusion twisting his perfect brows. "You sure?" He looks me up and down, taking stock of all the bruises and stitches in the daylight. "*I still want to kill him for what he did to you.*"

I smile, ignoring the twist of pain it causes and place myself into his open arms. "I don't want him dead." *Yes, yes I do, but I don't want you hurt more.* "It's just not the right timing."

The words fall like drops of poison from my lips, but he tightens his arms around me.

"If that's what you want," he murmurs, kissing my hair again. "I'll do anything you want to make you happy."

I snuggle into him, trying not to feel like the biggest liar in the world. "I know."

He checks his watch before sighing and releasing me. He peers at the stitches above my eye and frowns. "Are we still on for dinner tonight? My family will understand if we don't make it." His fingers trace the edge of the bruise and it's all I can do not to shy away from him. "We can call out for pizza if you prefer."

"With the pizza you eat?" I think of the disgusting pizza he made me try not that long ago. "No way. Besides, the fancy risotto always makes me feel better."

"Okay." His face softens, but his eyes still hold concern. "I need to go to work now. Are you going to be all right here alone?"

"You can't stay?" The question comes out more like the plea of a small child and I feel embarrassed when he frowns.

"These lawsuits... they could be bad. I need to find out exactly what is happening." The muscles of his jaw tighten slightly. "I can stay if you need me to, but--"

"No, no... I'll be fine," I assure him. I can't be the reason for any more trouble on his part. "Promise. You go get things fixed and we'll have a nice dinner later."

"I love you, Vesper." His eyes tell me it's true.

"I love you, Bond."

$\mathcal{A}$s soon as Dante is out the door, I sit down at the piano bench. Even Dante's touches couldn't comfort me like the piano does. I touch the ivory keys, and then begin to play. I don't even know what I'm playing or how long I play for, I just let the music flow through me.

Every time I think of Dante, the melody is beautiful. Every time I think of Norwood, I lose focus, and the music becomes terrible. Just like my life. Still, the piano is soothing. It is the one thing in my life I can always depend on.

Minutes pass, maybe even hours. I'm interrupted by my phone ringing, but I don't even bother to answer it. As soon as it stops ringing, it starts again. I think of Dante, and the trouble his company is in. I sigh deeply, touching the piano one more time, like a lover. *I'll return to you soon,* I think.

I answer the phone. "Dante?"

"No, this is Dr. Robins from Urgent Care. We met last night."

Met isn't exactly the word I'd use for this situation, but it sounded better than anything else I could come up with.

"Hello, Dr. Robins. Is there a problem? I know my health insurance is valid..."

"No, that's not why I'm calling. I need to discuss a lab result with you." He sounds tired. Probably from staying up all night stitching me up. "I got pulled into an emergency and I didn't get the chance to tell you. The nurses let you leave without telling me."

"What is it that you need to tell me?" I ask. I'm suddenly tired again.

"Ms. Savio, I'd like to inform you that you are pregnant."

I don't move. I don't blink. I'm not sure I even heard the doctor correctly. "Excuse me, what?"

"You're pregnant. The test came back positive. You're still very early. Given what happened to you, I would highly recommend you make an appointment with an OB. You should have someone check you out." He pauses. "And if you need any help getting out of a bad situation, please let someone know. I have people I can put you into contact with."

"Right." I nod, even though he can't see it. "Thank you, doctor."

I hang up the phone and stare at it.

I'm pregnant. The only person it could possibly be is Dante's. Somewhere along the line we weren't careful enough.

My hands drift down to my belly. Thank heaven Norwood never hit me there. He wanted the bruises to show. He wanted to humiliate me, so he didn't hit my stomach. It was a blessing in disguise.

He didn't know it, but he'd spared my baby's life.

I sit on my bed in shock. I'm going to be a mother. It makes me think of my own mother. I wonder what she would think. She'd probably be mad that I wasn't married yet. She would probably be excited.

I look back at the piano. My mother. I'm going to be a mother. It still doesn't feel real yet. I see Nan's bible sitting on the bookshelf. I wonder if my child will carry this large, heavy book through their life like I did mine.

I am about to reach for the book, but the phone rings. I half expect it to be the doctor telling me that he got the files mixed up and that I wasn't really pregnant.

But, my period is late. My breasts hurt even before last night, and I had been so tired the last few days.

The phone buzzes in my hands and I quickly pick it up.

"Hello?"

"Hey, it's Sara. Are we still on for breakfast this morning?"

"Sara, I'm sorry, I forgot all about it."

"Well, hurry your ass down here. I'm getting hungry waiting for you."

"Sara, I-" I try to tell her that I'm not coming, but she has already hung up. I smile. That's part of why I like her so much. Like me, she doesn't take shit from anyone.

I consider not going down anyway, but I could use some fresh air. Ethan has given me a panic button to carry with me as well as pepper spray. I feel a little safer having them with me, even just going downstairs. I throw on some sweats and a little makeup to cover the bruises and make my way down to the diner.

As soon as Sara sees me, I can practically see her hackles go up.

"Did *he* do this to you?" she asks immediately. I shake my head. "You can tell me if he did. Nobody gets away with hurting my Cara like this."

"It wasn't Dante," I say. Already the few other patrons in the diner were looking our way. I dislike the fact that she drew so much attention to me, and I'm glad when I'm able to duck into a booth, away from their prying eyes.

"Well then, who was it?"

I sigh. I'm not sure I want to go into it all right now. I don't want to talk about Norwood. I don't want to talk about the pregnancy until I've told Dante.

"It's complicated," I tell her. "Be kind to Ethan. He feels terrible about letting me walk into a bad situation."

"That's why he was so moody." She slouches back in her chair. "He wouldn't talk to me at all last night or this morning. What happened?"

"I decided to be macho and go into a meeting without backup," I tell her. "It was a bad decision."

"I'm so sorry, Cara. If you need me to help..."

"It's okay. I'll be fine. Just know that I'll be seeing a lot more of your boyfriend. I'm not going anywhere without him for a while."

"Hell, I'll go with you too. No one messes with my friends."

I smile at her. She's making me feel better already. "I want pancakes."

"Okay." She shrugs. "I actually have news for you. Good news."

I wave to a waitress. Suddenly, I'm starving for pancakes. With syrup. It's probably the pregnancy.

"Good news?" I ask her as I wait for the waitress. Sara grins.

"I'll tell you after we order."

I quickly give my order for pancakes with extra syrup to the waitress. Sara orders just some scrambled eggs. The idea of eggs makes me queasy.

Once the waitress leaves I make a show of focusing on Sara. "Okay. What's the good news?"

"I did some digging," Sara starts. "It's actually impressive how much a pretty face and bar tab will get you."

I frown, not really understanding. Sara was gorgeous. That's why she modeled in New York after all, but I wasn't sure why that mattered to me.

"I went to Red's down on fourth street."

"You went to Red's? That's Romano territory." My concern suddenly goes up.

"Don't worry," she says quickly. "I made sure I was safe. Ethan got me one of the Romano cousins who owes him a favor to watch out for me."

"Sara, I don't want you risking yourself for me..." I shake my head.

"I know. But, I have to tell you what I learned." She grins and I can't stay mad at her.

"What?"

"Victoria made a deal with Mrs. Romano that Dante would marry their daughter, Candy," Sara explained.

"Why would she do that? Candy is two years older than Dante and I'm pretty sure she's gay."

"It's what Mrs. Romano wants. She's not really interested in what her daughter wants," Sara explains. "She's wants her daughter married and respectable."

"What does Victoria get out of it?" I try to think of what the Russos would get from joining the two families. The Romanos were fairly small potatoes, but vicious. They weren't a family I would want to mess around with. They were a family we did as little business as possible with. Shady and dangerous were their best traits.

"This is the best part." Sara grins like she knows what all the Christmas presents are going to be. "It took me a lot of flirting to get this. And a pretty hefty bar tab."

"Consider me totally impressed." I want to know now. I want to know what she found out. "Tell me."

"Victoria Russo is being blackmailed by Mrs. Romano. Mrs. Romano caught her sleeping with George Romano Jr."

It takes me a second to comprehend what I just heard. "She was caught sleeping with an eighteen year old kid?"

Several of the restaurant patrons turn and frown at me. I don't really care.

Sara looks smug as hell. "Yup. It's a total Mrs. Robinson affair. I think it's gross, but then I'm not a horny eighteen-year old boy willing to shack up with a woman my mother's age either."

I can feel my mouth drop open. "Holy shit."

"I know, right?" Sara grins. "Apparently, Mrs. Romano found pictures of them on their security system. If Dante doesn't marry her daughter, she gives those dirty pictures to Mr. Russo."

"Holy shit," I repeat.

"Oh, it gets even better." She composes herself. "Ethan found this part out. Apparently, things haven't been so good at the Russo household. Divorce has been mentioned, and given the pre-nup, Victoria would get nothing if this comes out."

I don't know what to say to that. My mouth just hangs open.

"Keep your mouth open like that and the waitress will just set your food right in it," Sara teases me.

"That's why she's pushing so hard," I murmur.

"Yeah. She's desperate. I would take anything she offers you with a grain of salt. She's looking out for herself and is willing to do just about anything to stay in her comfy life." Sara leans back and puts her hands behind her head.

"You are amazing," I tell her. "Absolutely amazing."

"I know." She grins. "When you're head of the family, you can hire me. Or something."

"Done."

We both giggle. I have no idea what I would hire her for. Once word gets out that she's dating Ethan, no one will let her sneak into bars and get information. They'll all be too busy being polite so Ethan doesn't beat them to a pulp.

"That means she probably doesn't have anything on my mom, though." I feel a little sad. I had seriously considered her offer of information for at least a couple of seconds. Even if I didn't take it, I still liked the idea that there was proof out there that my mother's death wasn't an accident.

"It's pretty well known that the Savio sister's death is something you all have a soft spot for. Your uncle's apparently spent a fortune trying to prove Norwood had something to do with it, but the guys so slippery nothing sticks. It's not for lack of trying. Norwood just has intimidation and longstanding relationships with the police department on his side."

"Norwood has a lot of things on his side." I carefully touch one of the many healing bruises.

Sara looks at me, her eyes concerned. "You going to be okay?"

I nod. "Yeah. At least I know what's going on with Victoria Russo now. Thank you for that."

She shrugs like it's nothing, but I can see the small proud smile.

"Breakfast is my treat," I tell her.

She grins. "See? I knew I'd get paid back for it."

Just then the waitress brings my pancakes and Sara's eggs. Her eggs make my stomach roll a little, so I just focus on my pancakes. My mind goes a million miles a minute as I digest what I just learned.

I know I can use this. I just have to figure out how.

CHAPTER 24

I walk slowly up the stairs to my apartment after lunch. I had hoped that seeing Sara would make me feel more like myself, but it had only partially worked. Just because I knew what was motivating Victoria Russo didn't mean that she wasn't still dangerous.

She was a woman fighting for her lavish lifestyle and I was in the way. I needed to come up with a plan. I needed to call a doctor. I needed to figure out what the hell I was going to do with Norwood in town. I like having my panic button, but that's a band aide. I need a solution.

At least she got me answers, I think as I open my apartment door. I shrug and turn to lock it behind me. There's a sticky note taped to the inside lock with just two words written on it.

Good Girl.

I know that handwriting. The loop on the G is forever burned into my memory from long ago. Panic wells up from the acid pit of my stomach and I bite down a scream.

John Norwood was in my home. My sanctuary. My greatest tormentor was in my most safe place. He was here.

I go to the bedroom and strip the bed, putting the sheets in the washing machine with the hottest water I can set. I don't know what else he's touched in my house, but I have to get anything that might have even the smallest trace of him out of my life. I go to the closet and start ripping everything down and stuffing what I can in the washing machine with the sheets and throwing everything else in the tub to hand wash.

My hands shake as I search for the bleach under the kitchen sink and start scrubbing every non-porous surface I can find. I don't want even his fingerprints in my house.

Terror is making me sweat. All the progress I've made, all the strength I've accumulated the last ten years is gone. He stole it from me like he stole my youth. I can't get away from him, no matter how hard I try. There is no escape from him. *He was in my house!*

The phone rings. I don't want to answer it, but I know if it is Mr. Norwood he'll be even angrier with me if I don't. I don't dare miss his call for fear of what he'll do to me. Or Dante.

"Hello?" I'm far too proud that my voice doesn't shake.

"Cara," a familiar female voice greets me. It's not him. It's Dante's mother. I can breathe again.

"Hello, Mrs. Russo." The fact that I'm relieved to be talking to her is frightening.

"I was hoping you could join me for lunch tomorrow." The tone of her voice makes it clear this isn't really a request. "I was thinking of bringing Mr. Norwood to join us. I thought he would like a reunion with you."

Irritation overrides my good sense. I don't have time for her games. Not today. "You do that," I say, growing defiant. She obviously doesn't know how dangerous he is.

"You think I'm bluffing, Cara?" Anger ripples through the phone. "I want you away from my son. You are meddling in a world you don't understand and the implications of your actions are far over your head. You have no inkling of what a mess you have caused."

"Mrs, Russo, *you* are the one who has no idea what's going on." I'm far more angry than I should be about this, but it's a welcome distraction from terror. "I'll be happy to explain it to you at lunch."

I slam the phone down on the counter. I'm angry now. Angry and terrified. All I want to do is scream and then hide under a rock and die.

I crumple to the floor, rocking back and forth in tears. How can I expect Dante to protect me from John Norwood? Even though Dante's rich, and his mother is obviously someone to be reckoned with, John Norwood brought his company to its knees in a matter of hours. He could have seriously hurt my baby. I'm angry and frustrated and I don't know what to do.

Tears fall on the floor, but I just scrub them away with bleach. I wish I could bleach everything and just start fresh. But my life is never that easy.

A knock on the door surprises me. The windows are dark and twinkle with the lights of the city. I've been scrubbing for hours and lost time completely.

I stand and go to the door. I can see Dante through the peephole and I instantly am flooded with guilt. I forgot about dinner.

Dante smiles as I open the door, but it quickly fades as he sees the destruction I've wrecked on my apartment. It reeks of bleach and everything is tossed and scattered in my desperate attempt to erase any essence of Mr. Norwood.

"What happened?" Dante asks, looking around the room. I realize I've gone a little insane.

"I saw a rat," I lie lamely. It's the best excuse I can come up with. I don't want Dante to have one of Norwood's accidents. I couldn't handle it right now. "I hate rats."

Dante chuckles, apparently finding my neurosis endearing. "Why didn't you just call an exterminator instead of dousing your building in bleach?"

"I take care of things myself," I tell him. I wince a little. That's what got me the bruises in the first place. I feel the universe trying to show my a lesson, but I push it away. "Let me go get dressed and we can go. It'll just be a minute."

I hurry to the bathroom and pull out a freshly washed black dress. I catch my reflection in the mirror. I should put on makeup, but the bruises already ache and I don't want anything near my stitches. I pull my hair up into a tight bun and just put on enough eye makeup to make me look human.

I hear him lean up against the wall outside the bathroom door. "I have good news. The lawsuits are being dropped and the article for the Times isn't going to hit the papers," he says. There's palpable relief in his voice.

I freeze and my breath catches.

"You okay?" Dante asks, peeking around the door. His blue eyes are full of concern I don't deserve.

"Just caught a bruise," I lie. I smile, but inside I'm drowning. Mr. Norwood's threats are real. He wasn't bluffing. It wasn't just random chance that those things happened to Dante. Mr. Norwood caused them. I want to run and hide, but instead I just put on my work face and step out of the bathroom. "I'm ready."

The car ride to the restaurant is quiet. We sit in the backseat of a limo, our knees touching and not much else. I am lost in my own thoughts. I look out the window. The sky is clear with the lights of the buildings like tiny daggers digging into the sky.

Stepping out of the car at the restaurant makes me gasp. The cold burns in my lungs. I hate the cold so much.

The lobby is quiet, filled with warmth and soft tinkling music that is supposed to be soothing. If anything it irritates me further. My fingers tingle from the warmth after just the short walk outside.

A woman gasps. Heads turn and look at me as we walk toward the hotel restaurant. For the first time in years, I'm self-conscious of my appearance. I'm naked in front of their eyes and it terrifies me.

"What's wrong?" Dante asks, nearly running into me as I stop dead in my tracks.

"Everyone's looking at me..." I whisper, glancing around at the judging eyes.

Dante tips my chin up with his hand. "Everyone is always looking at you," he says. "You're too beautiful not to look at."

I pull my head from his grasp and shake my head. "They're not looking at *me*. They're looking at my bruises." I feel ugly. Broken.

I don't want to be treated like I'm made of glass, but at the moment I feel like I might be. And Dante is looking at me like I have a giant crack running down my center that might make me shatter at any moment.

My shoulders sag. I won't be good company tonight. Not after the past two days.

"I can't do this tonight, Dante," I say, defeated. "I'm sorry. I'm just going to go home and go to bed."

"Are you sure?" Dante asks. From across the lobby I see a woman whispering to her friend and looking at me. I can't decide if I want to burst into tears or go beat the shit out of them.

"Yes. You go have a nice dinner with your family," I whisper, looking at the patterned marble floor. "I just need a good night's sleep."

"I'll come with you," he says.

I shake my head. "I just want to sleep. And someone needs to have dinner with them. I know these things are important. Tell them I say hello and make me sound good. I promise I'll be okay."

Dante frowns, and then he sighs. "Okay." He kisses the top of my head. It's a tender gesture, but it's not what I need right now. "Call me if you need anything. Anything at all."

I force a smile and touch his cheek. He's shaved and smooth. "I will. Thank you."

I turn and walk back to the limo. Luckily, it hasn't left yet and I'm able to crawl into the backseat and curl up in a ball. "Take me home, please."

I stare out the window at the bright lights against the dark sky. Everything hurts. My hands go to my stomach and I cringe at how close it came to hurting this child growing inside of me. I used to be safe here. *How could this have happened to me?*

I remember how Norwood had treated me special once. He'd given me gifts. He'd taken my mother to expensive restaurants and always went to her concerts. I could see now how meaningless the trinkets of his love had been, and just how many bruises she had covered up for him. She'd tried to spare me the worst of it, but she wasn't hear to protect me anymore. I was so naive, and he had been so cruel.

The baby. I remember the flash of happiness when I found out. I still needed to tell Dante. I had gotten so caught up in cleaning my apartment and hurrying to dinner, that I hadn't had the chance. I closed my eyes and sighed.

The driver stops at my building and I run up the stairs. I'm going to make a cup of tea since I can't have wine and cuddle into bed and try to forget everything. Tomorrow I can come up with a plan. Tomorrow I won't feel so fragile and weak.

I open the front door, step inside, and nearly have a heart attack. Mr. Norwood is standing in my living room admiring my piano. One of Mr. Norwood's thugs closes the door behind me and blocks my escape.

"You're back early. Mr. Russo just not have the stamina for you?" Mr. Norwood turns with a wicked smile cracking his face.

"What are you doing here?" I ask. I wish I had some bravery left in me, but seeing him here makes me feel two feet tall and weak as a kitten. I reach for my panic button only to find I don't have it. I must have left it in the limo.

"Coming to see you, of course." He motions with his hand around the apartment. "I admired your apartment earlier, but I must say that the smell of bleach is not a welcoming scent."

My heart is pounding like a scared rabbit facing a wolf. "What do you want?"

Mr. Norwood crosses the room in two easy steps, taking my chin in his hand and forcing me to look up at him. "I can still see the defiance in your eyes. You think you are going to come up with a way to beat me. A way for your beloved Dante Russo to save you. You need to be taught otherwise."

He flings me away and I tumble to the floor. "I wouldn't..." I whisper, but I know as well as he does it's a lie. I'll never stop fighting.

"You are mine, little Cara. There is no escape from me."

He turns his back to me. There's a sledge hammer leaning up against the piano that I hadn't noticed before. He picks it up. Immediately, I know what he's going to do.

"No." I say, in denial of what I already know is going to happen. "No, no, no, No, No, NO," I scream, trying to get to my feet. His thug grabs my arm and keeps me in place. I might have been able to wrench free, but I couldn't take my eyes away from the scene in front of me. Panic, rage, fear, and horror splinter through my core all at once as Norwood brings the hammer down on the shiny black surface of my beloved piano.

I beg and scream as he keeps swinging that horrible hammer at my piano. The keys clang and the strings make horrible death cries with every violent strike.

The piano is my connection with my mother. It's how I bridge the gap to heaven and feel her with me. With every smash of his hammer, my connection is broken yet again. Twice now he has killed my mother.

The bodyguard releases me and I crumple to the floor. There's no sense in trying to stop him now, the piano is ruined beyond repair. Mr. Norwood drops the hammer into the rubble of my dreams and wipes the sweat from his brow with one of my drapes.

"Now be a good girl, or I'll have to come back." He pats me on the head like a dog.

I don't know how to be the good girl he wants, just that he wants me to try and fail. I know he's just going to keep punishing me, never stopping and never telling me what to do to make it stop. It's part of the pleasure for him. He can always change the rules to make me disobedient, no matter how hard I try to behave. He did it to my mother.

Mr. Norwood looks around, pleased with his work before walking out the front door and leaving me alone with my ruin. I hear his footsteps on the stairs as he leaves me. He knows there's nothing I can do against him. I won't call the police. I won't call Dante. I have no recourse to his destruction.

At least he didn't hit me this time. My baby is safe.

I pick up a white piano key, holding the marred beauty in my hand. Something inside of me breaks. Something that has never broken before, not even when my mother died. The darkest emotions I've ever felt have never even come close to what I feel at this moment.

Anger bubbles through me. He threatened my child. In threatening me, he threatened my baby. I will not tolerate this. I will not let him do this to me.

It is war now, and I am a mother bear on the attack. I now understand my mother's fury.

I stand up and look around with a detached sense of calm. I am in the eye of the hurricane of my anger.

The piano is destroyed. There is no way it can ever be rebuilt.

Luckily, he didn't destroy the small bookshelf with all my sheet music and Nan's bible. It still stands next to the shattered remnants of my piano like nothing ever happened.

A piece of the piano collapses, making a terrible snapping sound. I watch in slow motion as a piece of it slides directly into the bookshelf. Nan's bible wobbles and then falls to the floor.

"You need to punish me more?" I ask into the universe. "That wasn't enough for you?"

The universe doesn't respond.

CHAPTER 25

I stand in the middle of my destroyed room and wonder what I'm supposed to do next.

I'm not sure who I should call first. Dante? Ethan? The apartment manager? I think that I'll be staying at Dante's place tonight.

Just standing here doesn't do anything, though. I hate seeing Nan's book on the ground. It's always been in a place of respect. Leaving it on the floor feels wrong. I quickly walk over and pick up the heavy book.

A picture falls out of it.

I tuck the book into the crook of my arm and bend over to pick up the picture. It's of my mother, only it looks like something from a crime TV show. She's wearing only her bra and standing against a white background. There are bruises up and down her arms and on her ribs.

I turn over the picture and see her neat handwriting.

The date. A listing of the bruises in the picture and the name of the man who gave them to her and how. John Norwood.

My hand starts to shake. It's proof that he hurt her.

I frantically open the bible and find more. There are journal entries in her handwriting detailing the things he did to her. There are the doctor's notes with every injury and date. There are receipts to restaurants and venues showing that they were together.

My knees give out and I crumple to the floor. I stare in disbelief at what my mother has left me. It's everything I need to open an investigation to him. There's proof that he hurt her. It wouldn't take a leap of logic to believe that he killed her in a fit of rage and then made it look like an accident.

I flip through the pages, trying not to look too closely at the photos, yet wanting to see my mother's face just one more time. I make sure to keep everything as neat as I can.

Being in a slightly illegal business, I don't like going to the police, but today, I can't wait to give them this. With this, I have a chance.

I come to the last page of the bible. Tucked just inside the cover, I see a piece of paper with my name on it. I swallow hard, my heart in my throat.

She wrote this one for me.

My hands shake as I trace her neat letters across the page. It was with me the whole time. I had a letter to me from her sitting in my living room the entire time I was missing her.

I almost didn't want to open it. I didn't want to read the final words because I would never get the chance to read them again. There would be no more secret notes after this one. My mother could only reach up through the grave so many times.

I take a deep breath and close my eyes. I center myself. And I open her letter.

Dearest Cara,

If you're reading this, then something terrible has happened.

For that, I am so sorry. These are burdens that no one, especially not a child as sweet as you, should ever have to bear. I have tried to shield you from this as best I can.

John Norwood is not a good man.

I thought the first time he hit me it was an accident. The second, I knew that he enjoyed the power. I tried to leave then. He nearly killed me.

He said if I ever tried to leave him again, he would kill me. He would kill me and take my daughter. I cannot allow that.

I knew that if I was going to have any chance of escaping him, I had to have proof. I had to be able to show the kind of monster that he was to anyone who looked. I documented everything and put it here in this bible.

I want us to escape this life. I want you to be safe.

I hope that you are reading this because I simply forgot to take it out of Nan's bible. I hope that this time in our lives is nothing but a dark memory.

Know that I love you. I will always love you. The player may stop, but the music always lives on.

I love you, Cara.

I hope I can keep you safe.

Love,

Mom

Tears well up in my eyes. The letters blur and I quickly shut the letter into the book. I don't want to cry on anything and smudge it. I hold the book to my chest, hugging it tightly. This is my mother's words to me.

I have a weapon now.

Hope fills me like light from the dawn. I have a chance. My mother died protecting me. I will do anything possible to protect my child.

Fury fills me, but now I have a way to channel it.

I stand. The piano is destroyed, but I'll get another. I'll play again. This is not the end to my story, no matter how much Norwood wants it to be.

CHAPTER 26

It's snowing. The storm came in without me realizing it. Soft white flakes float through the air, coating everything in a silent blanket.

It's pristine. It's clean. With the snow covering all the danger and soot of the world, I can believe that things will work out. That there is a chance that I can bring this child into a beautiful world.

I stand outside on the street looking up at Dante's apartment. The light is on, so I know he's home.

It's time for me to tell him.

It's in the same building as his office, but higher up. I wave to the doorman. He doesn't question me this time. I ride the elevator, tapping my toes nervously. I don't know how he's going to react to the news that he has a child. I don't know if he even wants kids.

I know that he'll still marry me for the sake of our families, but I want us to be happy. I don't want to have a marriage of convenience. I want one that has love. I didn't know that until recently, but I do now. I thought I would be happy with just a marriage, but now I know I want love.

I want us to be happy.

I swallow hard as the elevator doors open. I step out. Everything is quiet.

I walk along the worn carpet to the door I know is his. My steps are muffled, but I still leave wet footprints behind me. I stand up straight, take a deep breath, and knock on his door.

"Cara?" He smiles as he sees it's me. His hair is messy and he's wearing an old t-shirt and pajama pants. He looks comfortable. The TV is on some old science fiction TV show. "What are you doing here?"

"I need to talk to you." My hands are shaking. I don't know if it's from Norwood, the piano, the pictures, or what I'm about to do. Maybe all of it.

His expression turns worried, but he holds open the door to let me in. He quickly turns off the TV and motions to the couch for me to sit down.

I sit gingerly on the edge. I'm a bundle of nerves. I want him to hold me and tell me I'll get a new piano. I contemplate just telling him about Norwood and waiting on the baby.

But, I need to tell him. I need to get these secrets out of me. If he's going to marry me, then we need to be a team.

"What's wrong?" he asks. His dark eyes are troubled. I realize that what I've said sounds like a breakup speech.

"There's two things," I tell him. I flash a nervous smile. "And I need your help with both of them. I need you to back me up and be my strength."

A little of the apprehension leaves his face. "So you're not about to break up with me?"

I shake my head. "Nope."

He sighs with relief. "Good. I think I could handle just about anything else."

"I'm not sure about that," I mumble. I take a deep breath. I open my mouth, but I don't know how to start.

"Take your time," he tells me. He reaches out and takes my hand. He gives it a gentle squeeze that gives me more reassurance than I thought it would.

"Norwood came to my apartment. He destroyed my piano and threatened me." My voice somehow is calm. Detached. I say it clinically, like it happened to someone else.

Anger floods Dante's face. Rage glimmers in his dark eyes. "I'll kill him," he growls.

"I have a better plan," I tell him. "I have a plan to ruin him. I don't want him dead. That's too easy. I want him to suffer. I want him to wish he'd never heard the name Cara. I want him to wish he'd been the one in the car accident, not my mother."

I say it with such force and spite that I shake. I help run a crime syndicate but this is the first time that I feel like a mobster. This is the first time that I feel like using my power to destroy someone. I feel dangerous.

Dante's eyes glitter. "Tell me what you want to do and it's done." I look at him and see a dangerous man. I've always known it, but now I see it. He loves me and he'll destroy Norwood with his bare hands.

"I have a plan," I promise. "But, I need to tell you something else first."

"Anything," he says.

This is somehow harder to say. This one catches in my throat. Telling him that I was hurt was simple. Telling him that I want to destroy Norwood was easy.

This, though, this changes everything. This changes us.

"Dante." I pause and take a deep breath. I look into his dark eyes, afraid that I'll see them change the way they look at me. "Dante, I'm pregnant."

At first he doesn't move. It's like he didn't hear me say it at all, so I repeat it.

"I'm pregnant."

He blinks, his mouth falling open.

"I thought we were careful, but..." I take a shaky breath. "You're going to be a father."

Dante lets go of my hands and leans back on the couch. Shock is the only thing on his face and for a moment I'm terrified all over for his reaction. This is half his fault. I feel anger start to heat in my belly.

"I'm going to be a dad?" he says softly.

"Yes." I keep the anger in check, but it's mixed with fear and hard to contain.

A slow smile creeps across his face. "I'm going to be a dad." The smile gets bigger. He's grinning. "I'm going to be a dad!"

He jumps up and kisses me, suddenly all excitement and joy. The anger fizzles alongside the fear, quenched by the flood of relief. He's excited.

He gently touches my stomach, his eyes soft and full of kindness. It's such a difference from the angry danger of before that it's like he's a different person.

"I'm going to be a dad," he whispers once more. He looks up at me and grins.

"So, you're not mad?"

"Mad?" He shakes his head. "How could I be mad?"

He kisses me softly. His hands cup my face. I smile at him, and somehow find that I'm crying.

"I love you," he whispers, kissing my forehead. My heart melts and I feel perfectly happy despite everything terrible that happened today.

Dante Russo loves me. If everything else in the world fell apart, he loves me. I could survive anything with that knowledge.

"I love you, too." I look up into his beautiful dark eyes and see the love reflected in them.

He smiles back at me.

"There is one small problem, though," he says, a mock frown crossing his face.

"What?" I can tell he's teasing me, but I'm not sure about what.

"We're going to have to move the wedding up. You're aunt is going to be so disappointed. She just booked the hotel."

I laugh, feeling my soul lighten. "I think she'll understand."

He kisses me again, and the world no longer feels like it's spinning out of control.

"I will keep you and our child safe," he says. His voice is full of hidden danger and love. "Tell me what your plan is."

I nod and tell him exactly how I plan to destroy Norwood and keep our baby safe.

 walk into Mrs. Romano's house like I own the place. My heels click with authority on the tile floors. I glide directly into Mrs. Romano's parlor and sit down in the chair facing her. I cross my legs and wait politely as she turns to greet me.

The first step to my plan is to take care of Mrs. Russo. I can't have her breathing down my neck and I don't need the distraction. Plus, it might provide some extra leverage.

"Cara Savio," Mrs. Romano says, turning to face me. She's around Mrs. Russo's age, but heavyset. Her dark hair is clearly dyed and she wears bright red lipstick that clashes with her skin. However, her eyes are sharp and bright. She is a woman who has done the mafia family dance for decades. She is not to be underestimated.

"Thank you for meeting me, Mrs. Romano," I say respectfully. "I appreciate it."

She shrugs like it's nothing, but her eyes don't leave mine. "You said you have business to discuss?"

I nod. "I have recently learned that you are in possession

of some rather embarrassing photographs of my soon to be mother in law."

Her eyebrows raise slightly. "And you think, what? That I'll just give them to you?"

I smile and shake my head. "Of course not. They are valuable. They give you leverage. I'm willing to purchase them."

"They aren't for sale," she replies.

"Everything is for sale," I tell her. "I know that you are using them to blackmail Mrs. Russo into giving you her son's hand in marriage. I'm going to tell you it won't work. Mrs. Russo doesn't have that kind of leverage over her son, no matter what she's told you."

"A mother's desire for her child is not something that is easily removed," Mrs. Romano tells me. She clearly thinks she still has a chance.

I decide to use my strongest weapon. "I can understand that. I'm about to be a mother myself."

Mrs. Romano does a double take. She looks down at my stomach then back up at me.

"Yes. I'm pregnant. Dante Russo is the father," I tell her. I smile and cock my head slightly to the side. "Do you really think that he's going to leave me, the mother of his child, because his mother says to?"

Mrs. Romano's face darkens. "I guess the photographs are for sale."

I smile, but it's not kind. I am the master of this situation.

"I can offer you money," I tell her. "And, I'll offer you something worth more. Mrs. Russo tried to screw me. I don't take kindly to that."

Her ears perk up, but her dour expression doesn't change. "And what are you offering?"

I give her a predatory grin. "Power."

Her expression moves from upset to interested. "Go on."

"I'll pay you for the photographs," I tell her. "But, I'm

looking to expand my territory. With the Russos and Savios combined, there's an opportunity."

"I'm listening," she says, crossing her arms.

"I want to deal with your family," I tell her. "I need more strength on the docks. We're expecting to move more goods with the marriage in place. I want to let the Romanos in as a show of good faith."

Mrs. Romano's face gives her away. Joining the Russos on the docks was the goal of marrying the Russos. The Romanos and the Russos both vied for the docks, but if they worked together, they would be unstoppable.

"Basically, I'm offering an alliance rather than a marriage," I tell her. "You get what you want. I get Dante. Your daughter doesn't have to marry a man she doesn't like."

Mrs. Romano strokes her chin. I know she's pretending to think this over but that she's already decided to to it. It's a good deal.

"I'll need sixty percent," she tells me. That's when I know she's in. It's just haggling now.

We're negotiating now. The fact that she's willing to talk means that the deal is on. Now it's just specifics. It takes some time, but we come to the agreement we both knew was going to happen

"Fifty-fifty. Whatever you bring in is yours and whatever we bring in is ours, but we work together and split the work," I say.

She nods in agreement. "We both win."

"Exactly." I reach for my purse. "And as for the photos?"

I pull out a stack of cash. It's mostly symbolic now that we have the business deal made. She takes my money and goes to a desk drawer. She pulls out a thumb drive and hands it to me.

"I wouldn't look at them," she tells me. "Not unless you have a strong stomach."

I take the thumb drive. I'll have Ethan check them and make sure they are authentic. I don't want to see my mother in law having sex.

"It's been a pleasure doing business with you," I tell her with a smile. I actually mean the smile this time.

"Likewise," Mrs. Romano says. "Oh, and as a gesture of goodwill, I have some information for you."

I pause, my ears perking up. "I'm listening."

"I know that you've increased patrols on the north side of town," she replies. "In response to the increase in unwilling escorts."

I wonder for a moment how she found that out, but if I could find out her secrets, she could find out mine.

"And?"

"Mrs. Russo is behind it. She needs the extra cash. The rest of the family isn't involved. Just her and a couple of goons looking for a quick payday."

My eyebrows raise. This is a surprise. "Why are you telling me this?"

Mrs. Romano's eyes glitter with malice. "That woman tried to screw me. As you said, I don't appreciate that."

The two of us smile at one another. This relationship will be profitable. Loyalty based on common goals is stronger than money, as the senator said.

"I look forward to working with you," I say. I mean it.

Mrs. Romano nods. "Likewise. I think we have a very profitable future together."

CHAPTER 28

This time I make the meeting with Senator Grayson. There will be no confusion. Senator Norwood won't be a surprise guest this time.

Still, I have Ethan and Dante with me. I feel like a queen with these two big strong men backing me up. I walk in front and they come behind me. I now understand why mob bosses walk around with security. It isn't just for show.

We meet at my aunt's office after hours. I arrive first with Ethan making sure that everything is secure as Dante and I set up in the office. We make sure there are comfortable chairs and refreshments. It feels rather silly to be playing hostess, but I know the details matter.

I sit in my aunt's heavy leather chair behind the desk. It feels strange to be on this side of the desk, but my aunt had insisted. I am running this show. I have to be in the position of power.

Dante stands behind me, his hands behind him and stance wide. He is my bodyguard. The shape of a Glock handgun is easily visible through his jacket. I know another smaller pistol is strapped to his calf and he has a knife up one of his sleeves.

He isn't about to let anyone touch me or his child.

Ethan stands outside my office like a bouncer. I don't have the full inventory of his arsenal, but I know he was just as well armed as Dante, if not better.

I steeple my hands and wait for my meeting to start. Outwardly, I look calm. Collected. Inwardly, I am shaking and nervous.

I think of my mother.

I think of her gentle smile and long fingers. The way the sunlight smelled on her dark hair after we played in the park. I remember her yellow sweater. I remember the loss of seeing her in that morgue.

"I love you, pumpkin."

This is for you mom, I tell myself. I will get justice for you.

It took ten years, but I am going to finally have the way to put the man who hurt her behind bars.

I smile, showing my teeth. I am going to destroy Norwood.

Chief O'Brien arrives first. He wears civilian clothes of a dark blue suit and pale green tie. He plays with the expensive wedding band on his left hand as he enters, but otherwise doesn't look outwardly nervous.

As a prominent citizen, it isn't that strange to ask him to come to my office.

He comes in and greets me, shaking my hand. He swallows hard before shaking Dante's hand as well.

"Please, take a seat," I tell him with a smile.

He sits, crossing one leg over a knee. "You look good in your aunt's spot," he tells me. "It suits you."

I nod politely. I can hear Ethan greet someone and a moment later, the office door opens. Senator Grayson walks in.

A little bit of tension leaves me. Despite it being irrational, I was nervous it wouldn't be him. The last meeting I was supposed to have with him ended with me being beaten to a pulp. I still have the fading purple and green marks on my face and arms.

"Senator." I smile and shake his hand. He shakes mine and gives Dante a polite nod.

I sit back down. It's time for me to start the avalanche that will bury Norwood.

"Gentleman, thank you so much for coming here tonight. I'm sure you're curious why I've asked you here." My voice is steady, but my heart is racing. "I have asked you here tonight to stop a criminal."

Senator Grayson looks slightly surprised, but Chief O'Brien simply nods.

"Senator Norwood beat and abused my mother," I inform them. "And I believe he killed her."

Neither of them show much surprise. It isn't really a secret that my family believes Norwood killed my mother. We just haven't been able to say it in public because we didn't have any proof. Until now.

I slide a packet of photos to each of them.

"In these folders are photographs of the abuse Norwood inflicted on my mother," I say. My voice shakes slightly. I hate those photos. My beautiful and talented mother deserved so much more than this. Dante puts his hand on my shoulder and gives me a gentle squeeze. "There are also copies of receipts, transactions, and what occurred for every documented bruise."

The senator's eyes go wide and he turns pale as he looks through the photos. He shuts the folder without looking at all of them.

"I know the chief of police where this occurred," Chief O'Brien says after a moment. "Statute of limitations hasn't passed yet."

"Good. I want the law to take this as far as it can go," I tell him. I turn to the Senator. "And I want these to go public."

A cruel smile crosses his face and he quickly masks it with an expression of concern. I know that inwardly he's doing happy somersaults. I just handed him the end to Norwood's presidential run on a silver platter. No candidate can come back from something like this.

"Are you sure?" Grayson asks. "These are your mother, after all."

I swallow hard. Dante has already asked me this question. Am I okay with pictures of my mother with bruises being public?

"She took these in order to bring him down. She died before she had the chance. She would want these to be out there if it means catching and punishing him. She took the photos and kept all the details so that this could happen. It's just that it's happening ten years after when it should have."

Senator Grayson nods, but I see the corners of his mouth twitching upward.

"There's something else I want with these photos," I say. "I want to push for a new autopsy of my mother. In light of the fact that the first one was done by a close personal friend of the man who beat her."

Chief O'Brien looks up slowly. "You're going to use these to open up her death?"

I nod.

He leans back in his chair and looks me over. "You think you'll get anything?"

"He was the last one to see her after having an argument," I reply. "He obviously had no issue with beating her. The police report doesn't match the coroner's report. There was no investigation done and it was pushed along. I want it redone."

"With these, I think I can make that happen," Senator Grayson says. "Norwood has a lot of people that don't like him. The only people that are loyal to him are those on his payroll, but these?" He points to the photos. "These will make a lot of those payments seem like not enough."

"You'll do it then?" I ask him.

"Consider it already done," Grayson replies. "I hope we nail him to the wall."

Chief O'Brien chuckles. "This is going to be a bloodbath."

"I certainly hope so," I tell him. He smiles a feral smile at me that makes me glad he's on my team. Senator Grayson wears a similar one.

"We're going to get justice for your mother," Grayson tells me. He smiles down at the folder. "Sweet, sweet justice. And maybe just a touch of revenge."

I feel a pressure lift from my shoulders. My mother will have her day in court against the man that hurt her. She isn't here to do it personally, but I'm going to make sure that everyone knows exactly what Norwood did to her.

I'm going to ruin his life like he ruined mine.

CHAPTER 29

The sun is shining and it's a beautiful, crisp winter day. The snow is still clean and sparkling out by Mrs. Russo's home. Beautiful green branches support fluffy white coats and everything sparkles in the afternoon sunshine.

"You doing okay?" Dante asks as we turn into his old house. Ethan is driving us today.

I'm meeting Mrs. Russo. The last time we spoke, she threatened to invite Norwood, so it's possible he'll be here today as well. Today, Dante isn't leaving my side for an instant.

"I think so," I tell him. Inside, I'm a mess. Just the thought of seeing Norwood makes my stomach roll. The bruises still ache from my last meeting with Norwood. My stomach is a mess of knots and I have to pee, even though there's nothing there. It's just nerves. Or maybe the pregnancy.

I think I'm going to be sick.

I pray she was bluffing and Norwood isn't there. I'm ready for an easy meeting.

Still, this needs to be done. After this, I'm free of Mrs. Russo. Soon, I'll be free of Norwood.

Then it's just Dante, me, and our baby. That's the light at the end of the tunnel. That's the hope pushing me forward when all I want to do is curl up in a ball and hide in a dark room.

The car rolls to a stop. Ethan hops out and opens the door for me. Dante is right behind me, his hand holding my arm and keeping me steady. The steps are carefully shoveled and salted, but he's protective of me.

I hold onto him, knowing that I will be safe with him.

The butler greets us and leads us to Mrs. Russo's study. We leave a trail of wet footprints down the hallway, but Dante doesn't seem to care. I try not to care as well.

The study is empty, as I suspected it would be. Mrs. Russo loves playing her waiting games. I take a deep breath and center myself. This isn't the time to get frustrated or lose focus. This is my time to take control.

Still, I hold my messenger bag in my lap like a shield. Dante is wearing his gun again. He doesn't trust his mother either.

"I see you brought my son with you," Mrs. Russo says, waltzing into the room. Today she's wearing a shade of green that makes me think of avocados. The dress is pretty enough, but seems like a style for an old woman.

"Mother." Dante says the greeting without any warmth in his voice. He doesn't move to kiss her.

She frowns a little but then shrugs his lack of affection off. "I hope you don't mind, but I invited a guest as well."

My blood chills. Today is going to be harder than I thought. I consider getting up and running, but Dante meets my eyes.

You can do this, his eyes tell me. *No running.*

"You don't need to look so worried," Mrs. Russo chastises me. "He isn't here yet."

That helps my chest relax a little bit. I don't have to face him just yet. Maybe I can miss out on facing him at all. As much as I put on a brave face, I am terrified of him.

"I must say, I'm a little surprised you called me," Mrs. Russo continues. She sits at her desk, crossing her legs. "I thought maybe you came to your senses."

"I actually came with an offer for you," I tell her, doing my best to smile.

"An offer for me?" She laughs. "You don't have anything I want. I, however, hold the secrets to your mother."

She tries not to glance at her son. She doesn't know how much Dante knows about her little scheme to me. I can tell having him here makes her nervous, but she is doing a good job of not showing it.

I open my messenger bag and pull out a folder. I fling it on her desk and it slides to her, but doesn't fall off the desk.

"Open it," I tell her. "It's a gift."

She frowns and shifts slightly in her seat before opening the folder. There's a series of photographs inside. I tried not to look at them too much myself, but I know what they are.

Mrs. Russo blushes a bright red as she recognizes herself in the photos. They are rather graphic and don't hide anything. It's very clear that she and a young man are enjoying themselves and one another.

She slams the folder shut. "Where did you get these?"

"Mrs. Romano gave them to me," I reply with a nonchalant shrug. "She and I have agreed to be business partners. As I am to be your daughter in law, she thought it best for our business arrangement."

Mrs. Russo's lips thin and she adjusts her collar. "Mrs. Romano gave these to you?"

"Yes. And she said you don't need to worry about her

anymore." I frown and reach into my bag. "However, you do need to worry about this."

I toss another photo onto her desk. She reaches for it like it might be a poisonous snake. In her case, it almost is.

"That's a photo of you meeting with Paulie James," I tell her. I toss another photo. "And that one, that's Paulie doing some non-approved business on the north side of my territory."

I add a couple more photos to the pile on her desk but she doesn't look at them. Instead, she looks up at her son. "Dante..."

"Yes?" He puts his hands on my shoulders, making it very clear where his loyalties are.

"You have to understand...." she starts. She looks at the photos. "It's not what it looks like."

"You don't have to explain to me," I tell her. "You don't have to explain to anyone. I just want it to stop. I want it all to stop. No more games."

She slumps in her chair, defeated. She nods. "No more games."

There's a knock on the door. Mrs. Russo looks up, hope brightening her eyes. She has a backup plan. I'm not sure what it is yet, but I have a feeling it involves a senator.

The butler opens the door and in walks Senator Norwood.

I can't help it. My hands start to tremble. My stomach clenches. It's a good thing that I'm sitting down because my knees are shaking. The only thing keeping me from panicking is Dante's hands on my shoulders.

"Senator, you're early," Mrs. Russo greets him with a smile. "But, I'm so glad you're here."

"When you said you had someone for me to meet, I had no idea it would be with Cara Savio." He looks at me with those cold, dead eyes and I shiver. "Cara."

I hate the way he says my name. I hate everything about him. I wish that God would strike him down with lightning where he stood.

"Cara was just telling me how we shouldn't play games," Mrs. Russo says. She's confident again now that Norwood is here. She can see the effect he has on me.

"I happen to like games," Norwood replies. He sits down in a chair next to me. I want to run, but I stay where I am.

This is what we planned for. This is what we hoped.

My phone chirps. It's Grayson.

Turn on the TV. Channel seven.

"Do you have a TV in here?" I ask Mrs. Russo. She frowns, surprised by my question.

"There's one behind that painting," Dante supplies.

"Why do you want a TV?" Mrs. Russo asks.

"There's a news story breaking. I think it's something Mr. Norwood will want to see." I look right at Norwood. "Especially since he's fond of games."

There's no concern in his face. In fact, he laughs. "Turn on the TV. I have nothing to hide."

Mrs. Russo fumbles in her desk for a moment before finding the remote. The painting lifts and disappears into the wall, revealing a large flat screen TV underneath.

"Channel seven, please," I request.

It takes her a moment to find the right buttons, but when she does the TV flares to life.

Senator Grayson stands next to a police chief. It isn't O'Brien. The breaking news announcement on the bottom of the screen says this is happening in my old town. Grayson is in Michigan for this reveal.

"... These photos are being looked at for federal and state crimes," Grayson announces. "This kind of thing cannot stand in our country. As a leader, I am putting my own money down for a reward on more information."

"What is this nonsense?" Norwood asks, frowning at the TV.

Then the screen switches to one of the photos of my mother.

He turns a deathly pale as Grayson's voice describes the injuries. "All of these are attributed to Senator Norwood. There are more photos and evidence. This was not a one time thing. As to the brutality suggested in these photos, the police have agreed to reopen the death of Caroline Savio Jeffries."

Norwood looks like he's about to pass out. His hands grip the chair and he's lost all color. Suddenly, he looks old and frail to my eyes.

He doesn't scare me anymore. He's lost his power over me.

"How do you like my game, Senator?" I ask, keeping my voice sweet.

His eyes turn to mine, burning with hate and fear. "How?"

"My mother left them for me. I actually only found them when you destroyed my piano." I smile, but it's feral and dangerous rather than kind. "In a way, you showed them to me. I never would have found them without you."

His eyes narrow and I'm glad Dante is standing behind me with a gun on his hip.

"You're just like your mother," he hisses.

"Good." I stand up. "Mrs. Russo, as you can see, you have nothing that interests me anymore."

She looks like I've slapped her across the face. I just put her down not once, but twice in the span of ten minutes.

"If you'll excuse us, Dante and I are going to go meet with

a caterer for our wedding." I gather my things. "Oh, and feel free to keep those photos. I have them all backed up and on the cloud for safe keeping."

Mrs. Russo and Norwood just sit and stare at me.

Dante takes my hand and together we walk out of his mother's study. We walk down the hallway, following our footprints out to the bright sunshine world of snow and sparkle.

Outside the birds are singing. The world is bright.

Dante pulls me in for a kiss before we get in the car.

"You did good, Vesper," he tells me.

And that makes my day absolutely perfect.

EPILOGUE

My daughter is six months old today.

Her name is Caroline after my mother and she is absolutely perfect. She has Dante's dark hair and my eyes. Her smile is his, though and that makes me love her even more.

She was born on a hot night in July. I barely made it to the hospital she was so impatient to enter the world. If I close my eyes, I can still see the perfectly happy smile of her father as he held her for the first time.

Our life is good. It's not perfect, but it makes me happy.

I run an organized crime syndicate using a mattress company to launder money by day, and by night, I am mother and wife. Dante is a mafia boss, making the underworld do his bidding and also the world's greatest father.

My aunt and uncle have retired. They love to watch the baby when they aren't busy traveling the world. They love their little granddaughter more than I thought possible. Family is everything. They make sure that my daughter wants for nothing.

Our business is growing. Combining the families has

opened more business opportunities, both legal and legally gray, that we never could have expected. Business is booming. Our families are succeeding.

Mrs. Russo is nothing but polite. She takes many vacations away from us, especially around the holidays. We don't see much of her, and I am quite alright with that.

The darkness of my past is behind me. I no longer wake from nightmares. I no longer am afraid of the darkness when I am alone.

Senator Norwood is in prison. He is awaiting a murder trial for my mother.

Once the news broke that there were pictures of what he did to my mother and that the case was being reopened, his minions started to break. One by one, the people that once kept him out of jail came and confessed. His money no longer paid for their silence.

He had only purchased their loyalty for a short time. They had no reason to be loyal once the money stopped being enough.

The coroner faked his results. The car accident was a cover up. Norwood killed my mother and paid to have everyone pretend that it was a car accident.

The world knows it now. He is no longer a respected politician in a place of power. He is nothing now. My mother has justice. Norwood is behind bars and will never be able to hurt my family again. He's lost all his power. He's lost all his privilege. He will spend the rest of his life paying for what he did to me and my family.

Next week, my daughter will be the flower girl in Sara and Ethan's wedding. Even though she can't walk yet, Sara's nephews will pull her down the aisle in a wagon so that she can be a part of their happy day. I've never seen Ethan smile this much in my life.

I've never smiled this much in my life.

But, the best part is that everyday I get to come home to Dante. Everyday, I get to see him smile at me and have him call me Vesper. Everyday, he tells me he loves me.

I am a mob princess and I have found my prince.

Hey there! I'm so happy you enjoyed this book about the mafia princess. There are two other books of mine coming out this month, and I'd like to share a little from each of them with you. Read on!

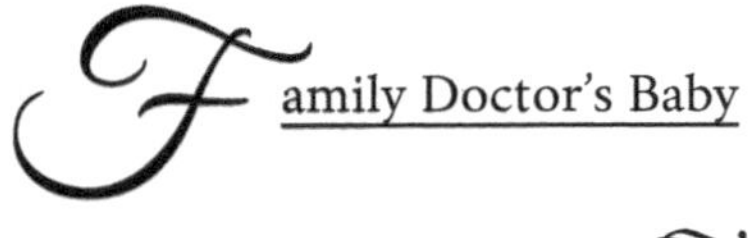

From New York Times bestselling author Krista Lakes, comes a sexy standalone novel about the baddest bad boy doctor and the sweet little nurse that he falls for.

When I left my small hometown years ago, I never expected to come back. I certainly never expected that when I did, I'd be working for *him*.

He's the town's doctor. He's supposed to be a respectable member of society, a pillar for the community. He's supposed to have come a long way from the bad boy who rode a motorcycle in high school.

But he hasn't. One glance from those lustful eyes looking at me tells me that he has the same voracious appetites that he did when we were younger.

Only it's not quite the same stare. It's more urgent. It's more intense. I'm not the same nerdy girl who tutored him.

I've grown up, developed fertile curves that I know he finds irresistible.

In this small town, rumors travel fast, and the family doctor can't be seen as a player. So he does try to resist. And I do too. But with every smoldering glance and moment of sexual tension, we find our barriers breaking down.

After a stressful night of touch-and-go baby delivery, a moment of elation overcomes our inhibitions. It seems like maybe we'll need to confront those rumors sooner rather than later, especially before I begin to show the results of that night.

Can I give this doctor the family he has always desired?

Dr. Matthews leaned in and brought his lips toward mine. He paused right before our lips touched. Just for a moment, though. It was as if he were making sure that I wanted this. The universe held its breath as we both held our breath. I noticed everything from the way his aftershave lingered in the air to the water droplets in his hair. After a second that felt like eternity, he leaned in the rest of the way, firmly pressing his lips against mine.

Our fate was sealed.

A soft moan made its way up my throat as I relaxed into his kiss. I closed my eyes and let my hands drift up toward his face. His beard stubble tickled my fingertips as I dragged them over his cheeks.

It must have been the adrenaline we'd both experienced that morning. Or maybe it was that the emergency had bonded us closer than ever before. I didn't know what had gotten into either of us, but I suppose it didn't need explaining. It felt good and right and that's all I really cared about. I needed a release that only he could give me.

Jacob slowly broke our kiss and dropped his hands to the top of my hips. Then he leaned in again, passionately pressing his lips to mine. My heart began to do flip flops behind my rib cage. Within a few seconds, I felt Jacob open his mouth and gently dart his tongue out, teasing it into my mouth.

A tingling sensation coursed through my body as our tongues lightly wrestled with each others, twisting around in a sensual dance. I reveled in the sensations: his taste, his smell, the way he held his body against mine. This wasn't a dream. This was actually happening.

Jacob broke the kiss and took a step back. His cheeks were flushed and his eyes dark.

"I'm sorry. That was unprofessional."

My heart hammered in my chest and my lips ached for more of his kisses.

"I don't care," I told him. "I don't want to stop."

He looked up, his eyes bright as they met mine. Desire that matched my own shone in them and my body heated. I took the step forward to bring us back together. Slowly, I brought my hand up and wrapped it around the back of his neck.

"Are you sure you're okay with this?" he asked, his hands already coming to my hips.

"Just shut up and kiss me," I said, still smiling.

Family Doctor's Baby

THE BILLIONAIRE'S BABY ARRANGEMENT

The Billionaire's Baby Arrangement

From New York Times bestselling author Krista Lakes comes a sexy standalone novel about a billionaire and the indecent proposal he gives the local barista.

Billionaire CEO Jackson Weathers needs a family for a PR boost, and I've signed a contract agreeing to give him one. A doting girlfriend in public. A wedding ceremony to invite all the socialites to. And finally, a baby for him to parade around, to show he's really a wholesome, down-to-Earth man.

I've tried to remain cynical about it. He's going to make all my dreams come true. So what if it's supposed to be a loveless marriage?

Only, his tenderness in private has me hooked. The way he kisses me drives me wild. When we make love, I lose myself to him. His body feels like it was meant to be on top of mine, like we fit together like two puzzle pieces. I can't help but begin to fall for him.

I can't tell him, or I risk losing everything. And nobody else can find out about our little "arrangement" or it will destroy his reputation. Still, I feel like I have to know how he feels, before the marriage, before the baby, before I give my entire life over to him.

Is it still just pretend?

"I was wondering when you were going to get home." Her hand went to the silky collar of her robe and she tugged on it gently to reveal just a hint of smooth skin underneath. She liked that he swallowed hard and stared.

"Work went long," he said, his eyes still glued to the bare skin of her chest. She let the robe open just a little more. "If I had known this was waiting for me, I would have been home hours ago."

She grinned and stood from the couch. She flipped off the light, letting just the pale glow from the city lights fill the room. With a grin, she undid the ties to the robe and let the fabric slide to the floor. The pale silk pooled around her ankles as she stood naked before him in the pale twilight. She knew the lack of light would hide her flaws.

His reaction made all the waiting worth it. His eyes dilated, his mouth opened, and she could see the growing bulge in his pants. She rather liked having this effect on him. She knew that he found her beautiful. She knew that he found her sexually attractive, but to see his actual reaction would never get old.

She felt like a goddess when he looked at her like that.

He reached out a finger and caressed the arch of her collarbone, his finger then tracing the curve of her shoulder down her arm. Goosebumps popped out along her skin, but it wasn't from cold. It was pure desire at being touched. His fingers caught the swell of her breast, skimming along the curve and barely touching her.

Her nipples hardened in front of his eyes. Hunger blossomed on his face as he cupped her breast in his warm hand, his thumb rubbing against the hard nipple. Jackson's pupils nearly took over the green of his eyes.

She took a step forward, threading her hand over his shoulder and into his hair as she pressed her naked body against his suit. She could feel the warm, hard spot at her groin as she leaned in, drawing his lips to hers.

He tasted so good. Every time he kissed her he tasted better. His mouth opened and his tongue quested into her waiting mouth, tangling with her tongue. His hand was still on her breast, playing with the nipple while the other hand went to her hip and pulled her further into him.

She pulled back, gazing up at him through long lashes and grinning. She rocked her naked hips into his, feeling him harden further. With the hand not around his neck, she grabbed his tie, fisting the silk, and pulled him in for another kiss.

This kiss was urgent. She wanted to feel him inside of her. She wanted his hard length to fill her. Heat was building in her core and he was the only one who could put it out.

He kissed her, letting her be in control for a moment. She smiled as she kissed him, enjoying the idea that the naked woman was the one in control of the clothed, powerful businessman.

He groaned, and his hand tightened on her hip. She wasn't in quite as much control as he let her think. He was bigger and stronger. His hip thrust into her, letting her know that he was going to fuck her the moment he had the chance.

And she was very okay with that.

<u>The Billionaire's Baby Arrangement</u>

186

ABOUT THE AUTHOR

New York Times and USA Today Bestseller Krista Lakes is a thirtysomething who recently rediscovered her passion for writing. She is living happily ever after with her Prince Charming. Her first kid just started preschool and she is happy to welcome her second child into her life, continuing her "Happily Ever After"!

Thank you for supporting an indie author. Anything you can do, whether it be writing a review, or even simply telling a fellow reader that you enjoyed this, helps me out immensely. Thanks!

Krista would love to hear from you! Please contact her at Krista.Lakes@gmail.com or friend her on Facebook!

Further reading:

Bad Boys and Babies
    Family Doctor's Baby
    The Billionaire's Baby Arrangement
    Crime Boss Baby

Kinds of Love
    A Forever Kind of Love
    A Wonderful Kind of Love

An Endless Kind of Love

Billionaires and Brides
Yours Completely: A Cinderella Love Story
Yours Truly: A Cinderella Love Story
Yours Royally: A Cinderella Love Story

The "Kisses" series
Saltwater Kisses: A Billionaire Love Story
Kisses From Jack: The Other Side of Saltwater Kisses
Rainwater Kisses: A Billionaire Love Story
Champagne Kisses: A Timeless Love Story
Freshwater Kisses: A Billionaire Love Story
Sandcastle Kisses: A Billionaire Love Story
Hurricane Kisses: A Billionaire Love Story
Barefoot Kisses: A Billionaire Love Story
Sunrise Kisses: A Billionaire Love Story
Waterfall Kisses: A Billionaire Love Story
Island Kisses: A Billionaire Love Story

Other Novels
I Choose You: A Secret Billionaire Romance
His Every Desire: A Billionaire Seduction
Wolf Six's Salvation: A Shifter Love Story
Burned: A New Adult Love Story
Walking on Sunshine: A Sweet Summer Romance
An American Cinderella: A Royal Love Story
Mr. Darcy's Kiss: A Contemporary Pride and Prejudice